The Dashing Widow

Elizabeth Bramwell

chinook
sun

ISBN: 978-1-9994096-0-9

DEDICATION

For my Mum
Thanks for talking me into this

Also by Elizabeth Bramwell

The Foolish Friend

His Darling Belle

The Rebel Wife

A Novel Miss

The Alter Ego

The Independent Heiress

CHAPTER ONE

As fond as she was of her elder brother, there were times when Lady Emma Loughcroft rather fancied strangling him. At present George, Earl of Gloucester, was pacing her sitting room at a speed that made her feel quite exhausted, and was yet to draw breath long enough for her to push a word in.

"St James Street, Emma! That... that hoyden you currently have living under your protection only went and drove your phaeton down St James'! And if that were not bad enough, she had the audacity to blow a kiss at the Bow Window as she passed it!"

Lady Emma sighed. Any sense of pleasure in seeing George was dampened by the fact that he had spent the last fifteen minutes listing all the reasons that her dearest friend and current houseguest, Mrs Abigail Merriweather, was not only the most appalling female that he had ever had the misfortune to meet, but also a scourge upon the genteel inhabitants of London.

"Honestly George, don't you think you're exaggerating just a little? I'll admit that it was a touch dashing of her, but I assure you she has apologised profusely for her actions. Most people seem to have taken it in an indulgent light, considering the circumstances, and if no one sees fit to make gossip out of it then I very much believe that it will be forgotten about within the week."

"Oh, do you think so? Allow me to be more up to the snuff than you, my dear. Good God, they'll be talking about it for months, and dragging the good name of our family into the whole scandal."

Emma sank back into her chair, torn between amusement and a strong desire to slap her brother. She laid a hand across her stomach, starting to swell now that she was a good six months into her pregnancy, and sent up a silent prayer that her child did not inherit their uncle's temperament.

"I do not see what concern that is of yours, George. Loughcroft thought the whole incident rather amusing, and is sure she'll calm down once she has been about town for another month."

"Oh, well that makes it all right and tight, then! I am sure that if Alistair Loughcroft says Mrs Merriweather's behaviour is acceptable, then there can be no argument over the matter!" he snapped, pacing up and down her room like a caged bear.

Emma rolled her eyes at this comment, and chose to ignore George's disparaging remarks about his lifelong best friend.

"Now that was unfair. I know that Abigail's behaviour has been a little wild, but it is only to be expected. She has never had a London Season, you know, and now she is out of mourning for her late husband it is hardly surprising that she wants to have a little fun."

"Indeed, Emma? Indeed? So you are not concerned about her friendship with every rake and fortune hunter on the town? And you cannot tell me that her petticoats were not dampened at the Cooper's ball, my dear, for I am yet to see a gown cling more indecently!"

"Yes, I noticed how fixated you were on Abigail's dress," murmured Emma, staring at him thoughtfully as he continued to list the various faults he found with Mrs Merriweather's character.

"She has a dashed uncivil tongue in her head too; you should have heard what she said to the Hardens at the theatre last week."

"I did, and Lady Harden deserved the set down. She may be our cousin, but she's an interfering old busybody who had no right to criticise Abigail's perfectly unexceptionable dress."

"Oh, do you really think so? And what about the incident at the balloon ascension?"

Emma's temper flared. "That was an accident as well you know, and besides which I had thought we all agreed not speak of it again. The only people who could possibly condemn poor Abigail for what happened are malicious, or jealous, or both!"

Her brother looked slightly taken aback by her outburst, but gave an almost imperceptible nod to acknowledge her point. Emma sighed, the anger dying as swiftly as it had risen. She shifted around in her chair in a vain attempt to get comfortable.

George's silence did not last long. "The thing is, Sis, someone like Mrs Merriweather is out to court scandal. I know she is a long time friend of yours, but that woman has been nothing but trouble since she arrived in London."

"But I still fail to see what concern is it of yours, George? Abigail is a guest in our house, and her actions in no way reflect on you or the Gloucester name."

"It is my responsibility to look after my family members, particularly when one is being taken advantage of by a vulgar widow who needs nothing more than a good beating!"

The door behind them opened.

"Do I, my Lord Gloucester? And are you the one who is going to deliver it?" asked Abigail Merriweather as she entered the room.

It would have been rather funny, reflected Emma, if the whole situation had not been so mortifying. George – who had turned an unattractive shade of beetroot – stood ramrod-straight by the fireplace, apparently at a loss for words for the first time since he'd entered her house. Abigail Merriweather was as graceful as ever, and nothing in her demeanour gave away the fact that she'd just overheard the brother of her best friend insulting her.

Despite the hostility between them, Emma was once again struck by the fact that they were a remarkably well matched couple. George was tall and well built with handsome, if somewhat sharp features. He had met Beau Brummell at an impressionable age, and as such was always simply but impeccably dressed in a well-fitting coat, pale pantaloons and shining black hessians.

It would be more truthful to call Abigail handsome as opposed to pretty, particularly when she set her chin in the defiant expression she most commonly wore around the Earl, but her dusky curls softened her features, her walking dress made the most of her figure and her cherry red pelisse suited her colouring admirably. It would have been an unexceptional outfit, were it not for the dashing hat she wore at a jaunty angle atop her ringlets. It was just the sort of ridiculous piece of decoration that would incur George's disapproval, as it was walking the line of acceptability for a lady of quality.

There really was no need for quite that many ostrich feathers. Or pink rosebuds. Or fruit.

As Abigail came over to plant a kiss onto her cheek, Emma steeled herself for the inevitable battle that was brewing between her oldest friend and her big brother. She suspected that George had noticed the hat, and did not think it would be long before his anger helped him regain the power of speech.

"I'm sorry that I took so long, dearest," said the young widow, "but I ran into Captain Rowlands, and he simply insisted that he would escort me home. I cannot understand why he is still unmarried. That man is such a flirt I swear he could charm any creature he set his mind to."

"Yes, particularly flighty young widows," muttered George. Abigail turned to face him, her movements slow and deliberate, before bestowing her most dazzling smile upon him.

"Oh yes, certainly them, but young widows have such a weakness for men in uniform, you know." She made a pretty curtsey, although somehow managed to make it appear mocking at the same time. "How do you do, my Lord? All is well, I trust, else I have no idea why you would concern yourself so much with my affairs."

George, much to Emma's dismay, seemed to have regained some of his righteous indignation as his embarrassment faded. "I suppose you would not, Mrs Merriweather, but as you have seen fit to prevail upon my sister's goodwill then the least that you could do is act with some thought towards her reputation. The lack of consideration you showed to her by your scandalous actions yesterday were outside of enough."

Abigail gave a dramatic sigh as she undid the ribbon under her chin. "There's no need to work yourself into such a taking, Lord Gloucester. If you're jealous because I blew a kiss at Lord Dagenham, then I promise that next time I'll make sure you're at the club before I set off down St James' Street."

"Next time? Oh, good God!' he snapped, and then stormed out of the room.

Emma watched him go. She closed her eyes and pinched the bridge of her nose. "Really my dear, did you need to provoke him like that?"

Abigail Merriweather smiled at her hostess as she removed her ridiculous bonnet, but her voice was apologetic. "That was bad of me, wasn't it? And to think, I promised you only last night that I would try to hold my tongue."

"I declare I have no idea why you seem so intent on baiting my brother," complained Emma. She paused as she considered his recent behaviour, and added in the spirit of fairness: "and I have no idea why he seems so intent on arguing with you, either."

Abigail laughed.

"No, don't you? I believe it is because he finds me terribly vulgar, and suspects me of encroaching on your hospitality. Both you and your husband, you see, are too good natured to turn a poor widow away, even if she smells strongly of trade and is single-handedly ruining your status in the Ton."

Emma smiled at that. "He is not as starched up as you think, dearest. I own that George is a bit high and mighty at times, but he has a good heart and he knows as well as I do that your birth is impeccable."

"Alas, but that of the late Robert Merriweather was not," replied Abigail. Her smile did not meet her eyes as she began to undo her pelisse.

Emma was at a loss for what to say. There had been one too many snubs, one too many balls to which Mrs Merriweather had not been invited, for her to argue with her old friend. The combination of her genteel birth and the trade-based fortune she had inherited from her late husband meant that plenty of young noblemen – and those who were not so noble – were willing to look past the origin of her wealth; but her natural charm and good looks meant that any of the Ton's matrons looking to catch a husband for a plain daughter wanted nothing to do with Abigail Merriweather, and were willing to stoop to quite vulgar levels in order to prevent the widow appearing at select gatherings. It was a good thing that Abigail had no interest in dancing at Almacks; even Emma's influence had not been able to win a coveted voucher for her friend.

Abigail looked up, and as her eyes met Emma's her expression softened. "Oh dear, listen to me going on like there's no tomorrow! I do not mind for myself, truly I do not, but for all his rough ways my husband was a good man, and he was worth far more than any of these minor Lords who think he was so beneath them."

"I know dearest, but you know what the Ton is like."

"Yes, indeed. Thank goodness Robert had the forethought to leave me a great deal of money when he died, or who knows what would have happened to me!"

That drew a smile. Much would be forgiven by the Ton if enough money was on offer.

"Oh somehow I believe you would have contrived, my dear. Now tell me truthfully; you are not going to repeat your drive down St James' Street, are you." It was a command rather than a question, and she was rewarded with a laugh from her friend.

"Of course I would not do so now I know just how scandalous it is, and definitely not after I had promised you! I only said it to annoy Gloucester, and it fulfilled my purpose."

"Beyond doubt," said Emma. She shifted in her seat, her hand moving to rest on top of her ever-growing stomach. "Why do you and my brother delight in annoying each other so much? It is not comfortable for the rest of us, you know!"

Abigail's expression immediately turned to one of apology. She crossed the room and sank to the floor at Emma's feet, one hand creeping out to rest on top of that of her friend. "Forgive me, I am meant to be making life more bearable for you, aren't I? Instead you've been kept busy teaching me the ropes, pulling me out of scrapes and scolding me never to attend public events ever again."

Emma laughed. "Well the less said about the balloon ascension, the better."

"I agree to that," said Abigail with a dramatic little shudder. "Although I think it very unjust that I am held to fault over it. How was I meant to know that someone would be foolish enough to untie – no, no matter! It is forgotten."

"As it should be!" Emma squeezed her hand. "I am sorry that things have not gone as easily as we had hoped here in London. I had thought that because of your own birth being genteel, that would be enough."

Abigail gave a little shrug, then said in a rallying tone, "Well there is no use getting upset about these things, is there? If I want the Ton to embrace me then I had better stop being a widow with a fortune in trade, and instead marry some titled gentleman of consequence. It would have to be a man of impeccable taste and breeding, who is able to keep me out of trouble. Oh, and someone whose own birth and social status is high enough that my first marriage will be deemed insignificant by the Ton. Now, who would fit that description, do you think?"

She pulled an exaggerated expression of thoughtfulness, before clapping her hands together with a small gasp of joy. "Oh, I have the perfect gentleman in mind! Is your brother perhaps hanging out for a rich wife?"

"Honestly, Abby, you are incorrigible!" laughed Emma, but in the corner of her mind a plan began to formulate.

*

George Standing, 4th Earl of Gloucester, made it to the end of Berkeley Street in a pleasant cloak of righteous indignation before doubts began to creep in. Although he was fairly certain that Mrs Merriweather had made it her life's purpose to goad him at every turn, he had an uncomfortable feeling that on this occasion she may well have had cause to be upset by his comments. As a man who was well known for his impeccable manners and who took real pride in the excellence of his deportment and behaviour, he found this feeling uncomfortable and somewhat unpleasant.

It did not take long for this small pang of guilt to turn to resentment; not only did that damnable woman act with total contempt for the rules of good Ton, she had the ability to make him lose his own composure with a lift of her little finger.

As he turned the corner into Piccadilly - still brooding over why, precisely, Abigail Merriweather was such a disruption in his life - he became aware of someone hailing him. He paused in his stride and looked up to see Lord Alistair Loughcroft, resplendent in a coat of blue superfine, crossing the road with a broad grin on his face.

"Hello George, Lord knows where you got that coat made but it makes you look a bit on the portly side, if you don't mind me telling you so. Are you heading to Whites'? Good! I'll join you. Have you been to see my wife, by any chance?"

George felt the corner of his mouth twitch, as though a smile threatened to dawn on his face. "I went to speak to her about the conduct of your houseguest," he replied as his best friend fell into pace beside him.

"Oh, you mean about Abby driving down St James' in the phaeton! What a lark that was! I never thought she would do it, you know, but the girl is pluck to the backbone. Cost me a monkey, too; last time I bet against her doing something dashing, I can tell you!"

George stopped dead, causing Alistair to almost trip over his own feet. "Good God, Loughcroft, are you telling me that Abigail Merriweather drove down St James Street for a £500 wager with you?"

Alistair sighed and gave a dramatic shrug of his shoulders, but there was real mischief in his eyes. "Not you as well, old fellow; I thought you would understand at least. Emma has already torn shreds off of me for encouraging Abby to do something improper – and deuced uncomfortable it was, too! And there is no need to start calling me Loughcroft either, Gloucester; I've begged Abby's pardon for leading her astray as it were, and she assured me that she didn't mind a bit and had rather enjoyed kicking up a lark."

George stared at his friend for a moment in utter disbelief. "Encouraging her to do something improper?" he echoed. "Alistair, you may well have ruined her reputation."

"You sound just like your sister," sighed his friend. "I mean with hindsight I suppose it was not the smartest of things for me to do, but how was I to know the girl isn't up to the snuff? She's seven and twenty, after all; I wasn't to know that she was unaware of the scandal it would cause. Still, so long as we don't drag it up too much it will all be forgotten soon enough. In fact, that was why I was looking for you, although I daresay that Emma has already explained our little idea to fix things."

George shifted uncomfortably, remembering the awkward scene in Emma's sitting room minutes earlier. "Well, no, as it happens it did not come up in conversation."

Alistair looked surprised. "Really? Considering the raking down she gave me over the incident, I rather thought it would have been a priority with her.

Women, eh?" he said, shaking his head with a little chuckle. "I suspect it went right out of her head; happens a lot now, not surprising since she's in the family way. I mean, if you didn't see fit to admonish over the St James incident, then there is nothing to worry about. Why, you're the highest stickler in town!"

George rubbed at his temples. "I swear, Alistair, I could happily plant you a facer right here in the middle of the street. I owe both Emma and Mrs Merriweather an apology, and you know how much I dislike being wrong!"

"Do you some good to admit you aren't perfect," said his best friend with a grin. "And if you owe the girls an apology that fits in perfectly with the scheme too, though I can't think what you could have done to upset them so. Lord knows why, but the Ton like to follow where you lead, even if that neck cloth is rather a sad attempt at the Mailcoach; you do know that it isn't actually supposed to look like you just clambered down off a mail coach, don't you?"

George ignored the jibe. "And your point is?"

"Other than the fact you seem to have lost your usual style? Really, old fellow, you've not been yourself for weeks, but there is never a good reason to be poorly dressed. Oh, you meant about the scheme we've hatched! Well, Emma and I think that you should take Abby under your wing for a week; dance at the balls, escort her to the theatre, take her out driving, that sort of thing. After a few days of gallantry everyone will forget about her blowing a kiss at the Bow Window," he paused for a moment, his brow creasing slightly, "although I suppose it might be a bit much to expect them to forget about the balloon ascension. I mean, I own that she coped admirably considering the situation she found herself in, and she showed a great deal of pluck in trying to carry it off, but not at all the thing, you know."

"No," murmured George.

"Still," Alistair continued, his face returning to its natural expression of cheerfulness, "if you're dancing attendance on her for a few days, then so will everyone else who wants to be fashionable, and I daresay no one will mention the balloon incident with malice. That way, we can both discharge our obligations to her, so to speak!"

"How strange that your obligations get discharged all through my effort," said George, although he was smiling as he spoke.

Alistair looked unusually worried. "I say, you don't mind, do you? Thing is I know how you and Abby rip up at each other from time to time, but I'll be damned if you can convince me that you don't enjoy the skirmish."

The revelation that Alistair had read the situation better than he had himself left George momentarily lost for words. Although his friend kept a tactful silence, his smug smile was not lost on the Earl for a moment.

"Be that as it may," he said when he finally regained his tongue, "but the truth is you've left me in a damned uncomfortable situation, Alistair, and I won't forget this in a hurry. I'll call on Mrs Merriweather later on this afternoon and ask her to accompany me on a drive around the park, but I make no promises that she won't fling it back at me and start another argument."

"I am quite sure that Abby will accept your invitation with perfect civility," said Alistair, failing to keep the smirk off his face. "And I also think that you might even find that you enjoy yourself, too."

George did not dignify this comment with a response, but as they strolled down St James Street towards the club, he was surprised to discover that he was very much looking forward to a drive with Abby indeed.

CHAPTER TWO

Abigail sat at the elegant writing table, taking the time to catch up on some long overdue correspondence. The pen nestled in her hand, the inkwell stood at the ready, but the sheets of paper before her remained blank.

The letters from her friends up in Yorkshire were all full of questions about her exciting life in London, and expressing hope that she was enjoying her stay. She hadn't the heart to tell them the truth, or to admit that she longed to return home. London and the Ton were not the fairy tale she had dreamed about, and the constant snubs from those who considered her to be beneath their touch was starting to wear her down.

She was just about to give up altogether when the door opened and the butler announced the Earl of Gloucester. She turned in surprise, only just managing to stop herself gaping as he entered the room. It had been less than four hours since their earlier exchange, and for the life of her she could not fathom why he had returned. She stood as he entered the room, even remembering to bob a small curtsey.

"My Lord," she said, proud of the fact she did not sound in the least surprised at his arrival. "I'm afraid that you have missed your sister, she has gone out driving."

"Did you not wish to go with her, Mrs Merriweather?" he asked after he had given his bow. Abigail hunted for some sort of hidden attack in his words but, unable to find one, consented to answer.

"No, my Lord, as she was accompanied by your cousin. I am afraid that Lady Harden and I find our friendship is greatly improved when we spend as little time as possible with each other."

George let out a crack of laughter. "Rub each other up the wrong way, do you? I'm not surprised. The old bat has a habit of being spiteful to pretty girls that take the shine out of that drab daughter of hers!"

Abigail blinked rapidly. Had George just complimented her?

"She seems to be fond of Emma, my Lord."

"Fond of the way Emma's patronage adds to her consequence," he snorted. "The Hardens are relations of ours – although not distant enough if you ask me, for they hang about like we are close family. The late Lord Harden was my cousin, and his mother my Aunt Seraphinia. Considering that Lady Harden refuses to speak to her mother-in-law, I find myself wishing that she would find it in her heart to feel the same way about our relationship. I don't blame you for avoiding them."

"Oh, not avoiding precisely, my Lord. I am shockingly behind with writing letters to my friends, you see, and it would be wrong for me to enjoy such a treat as a ride in Lady Harden's carriage when I have obligations to fulfil. She understood perfectly, although she did say how disappointed she was not to be able to enjoy my company for the afternoon."

He laughed again, and Abigail was struck at how much younger he looked when he smiled. Although she knew he had only just passed the age of thirty-five, his scowl made him seem a decade older than that. When he laughed in genuine amusement, though, he was a different person altogether. He seemed like the man she kept getting tiny, addictive glimpses of every now and then.

She shook her head; such thoughts led to dangerous places and she was too old to indulge in flights of fancy.

"Would you like me to pass on a message to your sister?" she asked, more to break the silence that had fallen than anything else. George stared at her for a moment, his expression blank.

"A message… oh, I see. No Mrs Merriweather, I am here to speak with you."

Abigail straightened up in her chair, lifting her chin just a little as she prepared for battle. This was more like it, she thought. Any moment now he'd launch into another lecture about her various flaws and faults. "Indeed, my Lord?"

He met her gaze and flashed a sheepish grin that

made him look absurdly handsome. Her breath caught, and she sent up a quick prayer that he was unaware of the effect he was having on her.

"It appears that I owe you an apology. Loughcroft explained the whole to me, and I hope I am man enough to admit that I had no right to say such things as I did about you. If it is any comfort, I am assured that Emma gave him a dressing down so thorough he thought he was back at school again. Will you forgive me my insolence earlier? I am truly sorry for having misjudged you, and I will consent to allowing my younger sister to ring a peal over me if it would make you feel better about the situation."

"There... there is no need to apologise, my Lord," she replied, her voice slightly faint, "I am sure you had only the best interests of your sister at heart."

She paused for a moment, and the temptation to tease him became too great for her to resist. "Although if I am completely honest, I would probably have driven down St James Street even if I had known how improper it would be to do so. Lord Loughcroft laid a monkey that I would not do it, you see, and I was honour bound to prove my courage as a result."

A strange expression passed over the face of the Earl, and Abigail could not decide whether he was about to let loose his temper or burst out laughing. She was not sure which reaction she wanted more.

"Minx!" said the Earl, but there was an appreciative gleam in his eye. "I can see quite clearly why Lady Harden and you should be kept apart at all costs."

Abigail laughed. "Oh I am not at all bad or rude so long as she keeps a civil tongue in her head."

"In which case I stand firmly by my earlier observation," replied the Earl, his comment softened by his smile. Their eyes meet, and for a moment the world seemed much smaller. Abigail was aware of a strange, fluttering sensation deep in her chest, as unusual as it was uncomfortable.

The Earl blinked, and the moment was lost. He raised his hand to his mouth and coughed as he turned his face away from her. "Horses," he said.

Abigail frowned. "Horses?" she repeated.

"I came in my carriage," he said in way of explanation. "There is a sharp wind blowing, and I do not wish to keep the horses standing for longer than necessary."

"Oh," said Abigail, and was irritated that she was unable to keep the disappointment out of her voice. "I suppose you must take your leave then, my Lord?"

"That would be the most polite thing to do, considering I interrupted you responding to your letters," he said, glancing over at the writing desk, "but I was rather hoping that you might accompany me for a drive around the park? Even with the wind it is too nice a day to be wasted sitting indoors."

She hesitated, the strange feeling swirling about in her stomach leaving her unsure of what to do. Although they did tend to argue on every occasion they met, she could not deny that a drive out with the Earl sounded like a lovely prospect, and was surprised at how much she wanted to go with him. The Earl, however, misread her hesitation. His smile became tighter, as though he was forcing it to stay in place.

"I seem to have upset you far more than I had intended, Mrs Merriweather. I assure you that I will not censure your behaviour again, whatever I have said in the past. The drive is merely a peace offering, if you would be so good as to honour me with the pleasure of your company for an hour or two."

"Of course I would like to go driving with you," she said, and was rewarded with a smile that set her heart racing once again. With a few words of assurance to the Earl that she would not keep him waiting above ten minutes, she half ran up to her bedroom in order to get changed. She tried to convince herself that her acceptance of his invitation was for mercenary reasons. To be seen driving with the Earl around Hyde park when he hardly ever took females out in his carriage was a guaranteed way to greatly increase her consequence, and possibly put out of joint the noses of all the matchmaking mamas desperate to snag the Earl for their own daughters –

particularly Lady Harden.

It wasn't the truth, of course, and Abigail was far too honest to convince herself that it was the case, although she wasn't sure that she wanted to explore her true motivations, or think about the Earl's smile in too much detail. As she did up her buttons she was aware that her heart was racing, although she was hard pressed to decide whether it was from anticipation, or from fright.

*

Drawing on his extensive experience of the power of a female to underestimate the length of time it took to change her clothing, George had no expectation of seeing Abigail within the promised ten minutes. He returned to his horses with the view of allowing them some exercise, and was considerably surprised when she reappeared not fifteen minutes later. He had driven his carriage around Berkeley Square only once to keep the horses from fretting, and pulled up outside of the Loughcroft residence just in time to see Mrs Merriweather descending the steps.

She had tied her spectacular bonnet back across her dark brown curls, and donned a beautiful green carriage dress with bright gold buttons that suited her colouring to perfection. A pretty little ermine muff completed her outfit, and she seemed rather pleased with herself as he pulled up beside her.

"See, I did not keep you waiting as long as you feared!" she told him with a flirty little smile, and George felt his heart speed up as she met his eyes. Much struck by just how beautiful she was when she smiled, for the first time he understood exactly why the match-making mamas of the Ton disliked her so.

She held out her hand to him, waiting for him to help her into the carriage. Her gloved fingers felt delicate and small within his grip. She stepped up into the carriage and settled onto the seat beside him.

"You can let go now, my Lord. I am perfectly safe."

George snatched back his hand faster than necessary, feeling as though it had been burned. He turned his attention back to his horses, and barked a command at them. The carriage pulled away at a faster pace than was decent, although Mrs Merriweather made no comment about this. They continued on in silence until the gates of Hyde Park came into view.

"My Lord, as much as I appreciate your reasons for inviting me out for a drive, I cannot help but think that if we continue at this pace, you are likely to create more scandal for me," said Mrs Merriweather in a conversational tone. "Far be it from me to lecture you on what the fashionable thing to do is, but I rather suspect that you are going to hit someone unless you slow down a little."

George swore under his breath, and then slowed the horses to a more sedate pace. They turned into the park, the silence stretching out between them. He could not understand why this woman could discompose him so easily, but he refused to use that as an excuse for continued incivility.

"I was sincere when I offered you my apology, Mrs Merriweather. I was wrong when I blamed you for the St James incident; Lord Loughcroft explained the whole to me, and I now see that you could not have known the possible consequences of accepting his wager. It was wrong of him, of course, but I hear that my sister explained the folly of his actions to him in great detail."

"Indeed she did, my Lord; I never knew she could be so intimidating," said Abigail with a chuckle.

"Then you don't know my sister half as well as you think," said George, sharing her smile.

"Poor Alistair! All he was trying to do was make my day more tolerable after Lady Harden said such horrible things about the Balloon-" she paused, her cheeks going red. "Well the less said about that, the better!"

"I fail to see what right Lady Harden had to censure you," muttered George, aware that his dislike for his cousin was growing. "You are a guest of the Loughcrofts, not of the Hardens!"

"Just so," agreed Abigail, her face schooled into

an expression of perfect serenity. "How perfectly rag mannered of someone to take it upon themselves to criticise my actions when they are in no way responsible for my conduct!"

Her set-down, issued as it was in such a bland, innocent way, could do nothing but appeal to his sense of humour. "What a shabby thing to say, Mrs Merriweather, when I have apologised to you twice already! Would you like to hear me say sorry once again? Very well, I am sorry for taking it upon myself to give you a rake-down over your conduct. It was, er, rag mannered of me, as you put it, and I shall not make such a grievous error in judgement again."

"That is very good of you to say, My Lord, and I accept your apology." She said with great dignity, but ruined the effect moments later when she glanced up at him, her expression mischievous, and added: "but only because I am sure that I will do something again soon to incur your disapproval!"

"More likely than not," he retorted, and they lapsed into a companionable silence.

"Thank you for this," she said after a short while. "You did not have to."

"I wanted to," he replied, the truth slipping out before he could help it.

Mrs Merriweather laughed, and the sound stung him. "Well, if that isn't the biggest plumper I've ever heard!"

"And you obviously know my feelings better than myself on this matter," snapped George, harsher than he had intended. If his reaction bothered Mrs Merriweather, she showed no sign of it.

"My Lord for the past month you have openly disapproved of my friends, my clothes and my general behaviour, counselled your sister to be rid of me, accused me of being on the catch for a titled husband and then accused me of using my fortune to attract every rake and libertine I can to my side."

There was enough truth in her words to grate on George's conscience and he began to regret giving in to the chivalrous impulse to invite her out driving with him. "I am sure that I never meant to give you that impression," he told her, aware that all of the warmth had gone from his voice.

Mrs Merriweather was silent for a moment. "My Lord, have I offended you?" she asked in a voice so meek he couldn't help but look at her. She had schooled her face into an expression of penitence, but her eyes were alive with laughter. He looked away, aware that the corners of his own mouth were beginning to twitch.

"Oh, alack!" cried Mrs Merriweather, pressing the back of her wrist against her forehead, "and I swore that I would be so good on this drive! Here you are, the great and gracious Earl taking pity on a poor, uncultured widow, and I throw back such magnanimous behaviour with vulgar insults. Oh, what is to become of me?"

George began to laugh despite himself. "You are a hoyden, my dear," he told her.

She smiled back. "Yes, but admit that you enjoy our battles. You are much too fawned over by the females of the Ton; you will become terminally bored before you reach forty. In fact," she said, sitting up straighter as though a wonderful thought had just occurred to her, "you could even say that I am doing you a favour by annoying you so much."

"Are you indeed? And how do you reach that conclusion?"

"I am preventing you from being tyrannical." She regarded him as he laughed again, this time her face creased in the most theatrical depiction of thoughtfulness he had ever seen. "I can see why this might be a difficult process for you. I suppose you are not used to having your will crossed, but rest assured, your future wife will thank me for my endeavours."

"Because you will have broken me down into a weak-willed man who will submit to her every request?"

"The best sort of husband, so I hear."

"Has anyone told you that you are a managing female?"

"All the time!" she replied cheerfully. "But I refuse to see it as a flaw."

"Perhaps not a flaw, but certainly not an attribute," George retorted, and he had the gratification of seeing her laugh. "See? Perhaps we can be friends," he said, hoping that he spoke the truth.

Mrs Merriweather grew very still, but the soft smile stayed on her lips. "Yes, my Lord, perhaps we can."

The urge to kiss her came upon him, and had he not been driving he was not at all sure that he could have helped himself. He reluctantly turned away from her, giving his attention back to the horses. He wanted to hear her speak his name, to call him "George" in that soft voice of hers.

"Abigail," he said gently, but she was not paying attention.

"Oh look, there is your sister up ahead, walking with the Hardens. I wonder where they have left their carriage? I am not at all happy that Emma is walking about on Rotten Row, she has the baby to think of. Who is that with them, do you think?" She gave a little squeal of delight as she identified the military man accompanying the three women before them. "Oh it is Captain Rowlands! Please pull up, my Lord, I have something I particularly want to ask the Captain."

The moment was lost, if it had truly ever been there at all. George obliged his companion by pulling up the carriage close to the Harden party, and had the small consolation of seeing the look of surprise on his sister Emma's face.

"Now this is unexpected," she said in way of greeting.

"I suppose that it is, considering the last time you saw us together we were arguing," replied Abigail. "Your brother and I have come to a truce, so you need no longer worry about us trying to goad each other." She smiled at the rest of the party, and civilities were quickly exchanged.

"My dearest Mrs Merriweather, you look as radiant as a goddess in that charming hat," said Captain Rowlands with an overly dramatic bow, further convincing George that the man was nothing but a rake. Abigail let go a small laugh at the man's flourishing, causing George to stare at her in surprise. Surely she wasn't foolish enough to fall for this, this scoundrel's false airs?

"Fudge! You can't buy me with your Spanish coin, Captain. Why, only this morning you told me it was too flash by half!"

"I was distracted by the novelty of being in close proximity to a divine being, fairest Juno! Now you are in your rightful place up on a pedestal, where I can worship at your feet. From this vantage point I can see the error of my ways, and rest assured that I now fully appreciate the beauty of your headwear!"

Mrs Merriweather gurgled out a little laugh, but Lady Harden, who was standing beside Emma, made a loud "harrumph!" which only served to make the widow laugh even louder.

Miss Harden, who had so far escaped George's notice, looked a little confused. "But she isn't on a pedestal, Captain; she's in Lord Gloucester's carriage."

The soldier choked on his laughter, turning it into an unconvincing cough. Emma looked amused, Lady Harden irritated. To George's surprise, it was Mrs Merriweather who came to the poor girl's rescue.

"Ignore him, Miss Harden; Captain Rowlands is trying to turn me up sweet with his nonsense so that I will dance the waltz with him at the Putney's ball. Let us ignore the silly creature, and hopefully he will go away."

Emma, taking the lead from Mrs Merriweather, changed the subject. "Such a terrible misfortune has befallen us, my dears! There is some damage to the wheel of Lady Harden's carriage, so we are forced to be pedestrians. Luckily Captain Rowlands here came along at just the right moment, and thanks to his powers of observation has spared us a tumble into a ditch."

"I cannot think why my coachman did not spot the fault," said Lady Harden in a loud voice. "I am quite put out, and shall reprimand him as soon as we return home. When I think what could have happened to you, my dearest Emma, I am horrified, and I beg that you will allow me to make it up to you; perhaps you could join my dearest Charlotte and I to take tea?"

"Oh there is no need for you to make up anything at all to me, cousin," replied Emma with a smile. "As much as I was enjoying the ride in your carriage it is always fashionable to be escorted by a gentleman in his regimentals, and Captain Rowlands looks particularly fine in his, don't you think?"

George kept his opinion on this matter to himself and tried not to glower when Abigail gave her enthusiastic agreement.

"How fortunate for us all, my dear Captain Rowlands, that you show to such advantage in a scarlet jacket!" she told him, her face a picture of innocence.

The Captain laughed, an appreciative gleam in his eye. "Fortunate indeed, Mrs Merriweather, and precisely why I purchased a pair of colours in the first place!"

"Did you really?" asked Charlotte Harden, her plain face creased up in a frown. "It seems like an odd reason to join up to me; could you not have just had a normal jacket made up in scarlet cloth?"

Emma and Captain Rowlands failed in their attempts to cover their laughter, while Lady Harden loudly told her daughter not to be such a goosecap. The poor girl stammered an apology and cast her eyes down to the ground.

Captain Rowland smiled up at Mrs Merriweather. "I am offended, fairest Juno! Did I not invite you to promenade with me this afternoon? You told me you were promised to your correspondence, yet here I find you accompanying his Lordship around the Park. Have I fallen from your favour, oh radiant goddess?"

George considered himself to be a fair minded man, and in that light he was able to appreciate the soldier's attempt to draw attention away from Charlotte Harden. He could not, however, approve of the way the man went about it, or be happy about the fact that Mrs Merriweather responded so easily to such vulgar flattery.

"How can you have fallen from my favour, when I was unaware that you were ever in it?" she responded with mock serenity.

The Captain held his hands across his chest. "You wound me, fair Juno! How can you be so callous and cruel to a devout worshipper?"

"Captain Rowlands I do wish you would stop with this silliness," said Lady Harden with a loud, decisive sniff. "It is no wonder that my poor Charlotte comes out with such nonsense if she is subjected to this kind of behaviour when we are out and about."

"My apologies Lady Harden," said the Captain, but his tone was anything but sorry.

"I do not approve of these modern manners," snapped Lady Harden. She had a voice like a ship's foghorn, only less musical, thought George, and gave thanks that she was related to him through marriage alone and not by blood. "Gloucester, we have need of you. Due to the damage to the wheel of my barouche we cannot drive back to the house, or return my dear Lady Loughcroft back home. You should do the chivalrous thing and take us up."

George tensed, and only the presence of Captain Rowlands prevented him giving his distant relative a heavy set down. Instead he contented himself with a condescending smile that had been known to make minor Royals quake. "I am afraid that simply isn't possible, my dear Lady; there are four of you, and my carriage can only take two more passengers. I am happy, however, to take up my sister and return her to Berkeley Square, and she can have her carriage come round to collect you all shortly."

"Oh, don't be silly George," said Emma, glaring at him in rebuke. "I do not have far to walk at all so if Captain Rowlands would be happy to escort me, I will very much enjoy the stroll. It would do you all good to remember that I am in the family way and not made of glass! You can take up the Hardens for a circuit or two of the park, then convey them back to Hallam Street. Indeed, it is the only decent thing to do!"

She placed a lot of emphasis on the last few words, casting him a look that only a sister could get away with. He relented slightly, consoling himself with the fact that he would get a further ten minutes alone with Abigail after the Hardens had been safely returned to their lodgings.

"My dearest Lady Loughcroft, you cannot possibly put yourself out in such a way!" cried Lady Harden, placing one hand onto the younger woman's arm in a gesture of fondness. "It is quite out of the question for a woman in your condition to walk all that way. No, Mrs Merriweather would be perfectly happy to give up her seat, I am quite sure. After all, she and Captain Rowlands appear to be on quite intimate terms already. I am sure she would get far more pleasure from meandering through the park with him than riding sedately in the Earl's carriage."

There was a horrible silence. Captain Rowlands looked as though he was about to explode, Miss Harden coloured up at her mother's incivility, while his sister simply stood there, her mouth hanging open in shock.

"Lady Harden, I believe that-" began George, intending to put the vulgar woman in her place once and for all, when Abigail interrupted him.

"What an excellent suggestion, my Lady!" she said in an excited voice, clapping her hands together as though she had been promised a high treat. "I have always longed to explore the more secluded pathways of the park, but until now the opportunity had not presented itself to me. I am perfectly sure that Captain Rowlands would be the ideal escort for such an adventure; I need not fear if I am in his company."

She hopped down out of the carriage, Captain Rowlands catching her as she landed directly before him. Something about the sight of the soldier's hand touching Mrs Merriweather's waist brought out the chivalrous lord in George. Either that, or the murderous one.

"Abigail you do not need to," said George, but she dismissed him with a wave of her hand.

"Oh you need not worry about me Lord Gloucester, it is a greater treat than I could ever have hoped for, riding in an open carriage with a real Earl. Now, Captain Rowlands, do be a dear and help Lady Harden into the carriage, we would not want her to catch her feet in her skirt and fall face first into the mud; lawks! How uncivilised that would be! Are you comfortable, my Lady? Not too cold? Really it was quite foolish of Lord Gloucester not to bring a blanket with him, but I suppose he was not expecting to have passengers of your maturity ride in his carriage today. It was remiss of him, but I am sure he will not make the error again. Now, would you like your daughter to sit beside you? Oh, how stupid of me to ask such a question."

She gave a conspiratorial wink that was clearly intended to be caught by everyone present. "I do think that Miss Harden should ride up front with the Earl, don't you? For Lady Loughcroft, you know, has the oddest dislike of being up close to horses, don't you, my dearest Emma?"

"Indeed," replied Emma faintly, apparently forgetting that she was a noted horsewoman famed for her love of good racing stock. She glanced at George as Captain Rowlands helped her to the seat beside Lady Harden, but he was at a loss to do anything but shrug. Abigail, who appeared to have lost all sense of delicacy, was chattering away to Miss Harden, and loudly instructed George to help the poor girl up to her seat.

"There, now you are all right and tight, and all perfectly satisfied with your positions, I am sure!" She gave a contrived giggle, then intertwined her arm with that of Captain Rowlands. "Don't worry about me, Emma, I am sure that Captain Rowlands is gentleman enough to see me home safely when we have finished our explorations of the park," she said with a smile, before half pulling the soldier along beside her as they headed off down Rotten Row. The Captain attempted to shout a goodbye to the carriage, but he was born off by Mrs Merriweather, and they were soon swallowed up by the crowd of people wandering through the park.

The occupants of the carriage remained silent for a moment. Although George was sure that Abigail's display was nothing more than a piece of theatre contrived for Lady Harden's benefit, he was not at all convinced that Captain Rowlands was the gentleman that she believed him to be. He swore under his breath, and was about to turn the carriage around and pursue them, when he felt a small hand touch the small of his back.

"Leave her, dearest," said his sister in a gentle voice. "I promise you no harm will befall her; she is more up to the snuff than you know, and the Captain is a good man."

He wavered for a moment; he might not like the soldier, but there was no way that Emma would allow her oldest friend to be left in the company of a man who would mean her ill. "As you wish, Emma. I will drive both you and the Hardens home."

"Home?" said Lady Harden in a demanding voice. Really, a foghorn would have been more soothing. "Why, it is not yet six o'clock! You should take us on another circuit of the park, Gloucester!"

"I am so sorry to be disobliging, my dear Lady," replied George as he shook his horses into action, "but following your recent misadventure with your barouche, I am unwilling to risk damage to my own vehicle, and will thus abstain from driving through Hyde Park until the mysterious threat to innocent drivers is disposed of."

He heard his sister utter an unconvincing cough to cover her mirth, but did not acknowledge it. He was polite enough to make and maintain small talk with Miss Harden beside him, but his thoughts were elsewhere and he was not entirely sure what their limited conversation had been about. He could not quite rid his mind of the image of Abigail sauntering along some of the more secluded paths of Hyde Park with Captain Rowlands, or of the soldier stealing a kiss down Lover's Walk, and chastised himself for not thinking to change places with the Captain when he had had the chance.

The moment was gone, and having to drive Lady Harden anywhere was sufficient punishment for his lack of action. He promised himself that the next time he met with Mrs Merriweather he would seize the moment, whatever the consequences turned out to be.

CHAPTER THREE

"Tell me, oh fair Goddess Juno, was that little show for the Old Bat Harden's entertainment, or was it for the Earl?" asked Captain Rowlands as the two of them continued their promenade.

"Do you need to ask?" snapped Abigail, her body still tense with suppressed rage. "Of all the hideous, vulgar and encroaching females I have ever met, Lady Harden is the worst of them."

The Captain patted her hand gently. "Now, now, my dear, we have been friends for a long time, so you should not hold back for the sake of decency. Tell me how you truly feel." He kept his face straight as he spoke, his whole bearing that of a man ready to leap to the defence of a stricken damsel.

Abigail let out a burst of laughter, which caused the elderly lady driving past them in her carriage to tut in disgust. "Richard, you are ruining my reputation!" she said as she watched the old dear drive ahead of them. She felt her anger beginning to die down.

"With all respect, Juno, you are doing a fine job of that all by yourself," he said with obvious disapproval. Abigail rolled her eyes.

"Not you as well? I thought that you of all people would have enjoyed the lark. I've had a rake-down from Emma, been chastised by Gloucester and then had to endure poor Loughcroft apologising to me, when it wasn't his fault at all. Lord, it was only a quick drive past the Bow Window!"

"I'm not talking about the St James incident – although now you mention it, that was pretty shocking conduct. I was talking about the little display back there. Lady Harden doesn't have the wit to understand that you were playing up to her insult, and will set it about that you're the type of female to enjoy passing liaisons with a red-coated libertine in the secluded sections of Hyde Park."

Abigail stopped smiling, a cloak of unhappiness settling across her shoulders. "She's the type of woman that would set that about even if I lived in a convent. She hates me with a passion, you know. Perhaps I should not have acted that way, but it is no more than she or anyone else expects of me. London is not the magical place I dreamed about, Richard. I miss Yorkshire and I find myself longing for the familiarity of Harrogate, where at least I have friends."

"You might not if news of the balloon ascension travels that far."

A stab of anger cut back through her. "Well, of all the shabby things to say! Did Old Bat Harden tell you about that?"

"She did, but it does not matter as I had already been told of the incident by one of my fellow officers. Everyone in London has heard about it."

"It was an accident," she protested. Captain Rowlands stopped walking, and turned to look down into her eyes. "Well, it was sort of an accident," she corrected. "I mean, I did lean into the basket, but I lost my footing, you see, and how was I to know that-"

"The less said about the whole thing, the better," interrupted the Captain. "I know it was an accident, but your enemies do not and you aren't doing yourself any favours by carrying on in this rackety fashion."

"You can talk," muttered Abigail, giving him a playful punch on the arm. "You've managed to gather a reputation as being a flirtatious rake and a dangerous fortune hunter. Lord alone knows how something that silly started up, but admit you've been encouraging it ever since."

"We aren't discussing my situation," the Captain told her with great aplomb. "I'm trying to tell you, my delightful Juno, that if you carry on in this fashion your reputation will be in ruins."

"I'm a rich widow," she told him with a sigh. "I'm also childless and young enough to remarry. There may be plenty of men who would willingly overlook both my reputation and the source of my fortune if it meant they would have access to it, but I suspect most of those who dance attendance on me have a very different type of relationship in mind."

"Are you out for a new husband then, dearest?"

Abigail snorted her disgust. "Not in the least. Don't get me wrong, Richard; if the right man came along then I would happily be a wife again, but it is not high on my list of priorities. And before you ask, I am not on the hang out for an affair, either."

"I would never have thought it! I know your conduct has been a little close to the line in recent weeks, but you can't fool me with such behaviour."

"The Ton is easily fooled," she replied, remembering some of the half-whispered insults she had overheard in the past fortnight.

"You're playing a dangerous game, Juno, and I have no idea what you are hoping to accomplish through it. The type of attention you are getting is not likely to win you what you want."

Abigail looked up and met his gaze. For a moment, it was as though they were back in Yorkshire again with her late husband and their friends, making her feel homesick in a way she had never expected. "I don't know what I want," she replied truthfully.

Captain Rowlands seemed surprised at this disclosure. "Don't you, fair Juno? I think I may know your heart better than you, and I suspect your friend Lady Loughcroft may know as well."

Abigail scoffed at that. "Well that's just a stupid presumption on your part, and on Emma's. How could you possibly know what I want, if I don't know it myself?"

"Because sometimes you should credit people with being more up to the snuff than you are. You might be seven and twenty, my dear, but you're still a child in my book."

"Says the doddery old fool of nine and twenty," she retorted, but smiled as she did so.

He had the good grace to smile back. "At least I know what I want, my dear, even if I am yet to find a way of winning it. However I am not entirely sure why you came to London at all, when you seemed happy when I last saw you in Harrogate."

Abigail sighed. "I don't know. A change of scene, I suppose. My mourning period was over, and I was at a bit of a loss as to what to do with myself. When Emma begged me to come to London I thought it would be a nice distraction for a while. I never had a Season, you see; I suppose I let myself get swept away in a girlish daydream of balls and rout-parties."

"Reality never does live up to the dream, does it, dearest?" said the Captain, his tone sympathetic. "Perhaps we should have both stuck to Harrogate and York."

They left the park, crossing over into Mount Street and continuing their walk to the Loughcroft residence on Berkeley Square.

"Well, no use crying over it," said Abigail with a little shake, determined to get rid of the melancholy that threatened to consume her. "The Loughcrofts have been darlings, and I have enjoyed much of my time here." She gave his arm a little squeeze. "Running into old friends has definitely made it more bearable for me, too. I almost forgot, I wanted to ask you something!"

"Ask me for anything and it is yours."

"Are you attending the Putney's ball on Friday? Emma thinks it will be a squeeze, for whatever people may say about Sir Joseph's bluff ways, they are a kind couple and very much liked, so no one in their right mind will turn down an invitation. Unfortunately, that means it is going to be full of Lady Harden's cronies and a veritable wolf pack of matchmaking Mamas, not one of whom like me above half."

"And you are wondering if I will come along as your cisibeo-in-chief," finished Captain Rowlands with a little groan that made Abigail laugh again.

"Well everyone thinks you are a rake, and that I am fast. We are the perfect partnership!"

"Not for anyone else would I put myself through such torture, fair Juno," he told her. "How fortunate that Lady Putney's son is a fellow officer and saw fit to invite the entire Regiment to her ball, else I would not have been able to keep you company. Shall I ask Harry and Percy to dance attendance on you as well?"

Abigail laughed again. "No need for that – at least, not unless we get desperate."

They reached the Loughcroft house, and the Captain handed Abigail up the steps. She turned back to him as she reached the doorway, stretching out her hand.

"You are a dear, dear friend, Richard. If there is ever anything I can do to help you, rest assured that all you need do is ask."

The Captain took her hand and kissed her fingers with old fashioned courtesy. "I may take you up on that in the near future, my dear Mrs Merriweather," he told her with a small smile. He bowed and walked away before she could respond, leaving her to ponder the meaning of his words as she stepped up into the house.

*

"Of all the hideous, vulgar and encroaching females I have ever met, Lady Harden is the worst of them," said Emma with considerable venom that evening. The outburst came not five minutes after Abigail had retired to bed early, and appeared to take her husband somewhat by surprise.

51

"Well I knew you didn't like your cousin above half, my love, and Lord knows I can barely stand the woman, but I wouldn't say she was quite as bad as that," replied Alistair as he poured himself a glass of brandy.

"You didn't hear what she said to poor Abby in Hyde Park," said Emma, before recounting the events of the promenade. "Why, she might as well have called her a lightskirt!"

"Dashed uncivil of her, I must say. I wondered why Abby seemed a touch out of sorts at dinner. Not like her to plead a headache and head up to bed early."

"No, not at all, which is why I expect this whole business has upset her far more than she will admit to me. Ooh, I could strangle that dratted cousin of mine. She took Abby in dislike from the moment I introduced them, you know, and has done nothing but spread poison about her ever since."

"I always said Old Bat Harden had a nasty tongue in her head."

"I just don't understand why she hates Abby so much."

Alistair looked up from his drink in surprise. "Don't you, my love?"

"Well of course not. Abigail may have kicked up a few too many larks over the last few weeks, but they were only in response to her treatment. She was as good as gold when she first came to London, I even thought she might become a hit with the Ton."

"So did Lady Harden and her cronies."

Emma blinked. "I don't understand."

"They've got daughters," said Alistair as though it explained everything. Emma stared at him expectantly, and he gave a sigh. "Some of them girls are as plain as unbuttered bread. Even the pretty ones don't have much in the way of fortune. Stands to reason they wouldn't want Abby around, she takes the shine out of them."

"I suppose I can understand that," conceded Emma. "But Abby is very wealthy in her own right, and besides, she isn't looking for a husband."

"Also part of the problem," murmured Alistair before taking a sip of his brandy.

"How would that be a problem?" asked Emma, somewhat perplexed. "And it also doesn't explain why some of the matrons who don't even have daughters have been cool with her."

Alistair, realising he was on dangerous ground, choked on his drink. "Oh nothing, nothing!"

Emma crossed her arms over her stomach and glared at him. It was less than a minute before he gave up trying to ignore her and answered the question.

"Might not be worried about Abby taking the shine from an unmarried daughter, my love, but they'll be worried about her catching the eye of their sons or, more specifically, their husbands."

Emma's mouth dropped open. "Do they really, Alistair? Well of all the silly things to think! It just goes to show how unfair and uncivil they are being. I mean, I am perfectly aware of how much you admire and like Abigail, yet I'm not worried about anything of that nature happening under this roof. If I have no concerns, why should they?"

Alistair looked her over with an adoring gaze. He reached out to envelop her hand in his, raising it to his lips for a lingering kiss. "May be due to the fact that it's well known I'm unfashionably in love with my wife."

Emma blushed. "I am lucky, aren't I?" she said impulsively.

"Not a bit of it!" Alistair told her with a smile. "If you don't believe me, ask your brother! He'll point out to you all the better offers for your hand that you received. Reminds me about them often enough."

She laughed, but the mention of her brother turned her thoughts back to Abigail.

"Do you know, I think that George was quite put out when Abby went walking with the Captain."

"Stands to reason. I'd be put out if I had to drive about with the Hardens instead of Abby."

"Well yes, but that's not what I meant. It was almost as if he was, well, almost jealous of the Captain. You know, I've been thinking about that-"

Alistair's sense of self-preservation kicked in. He sat up straight in his chair and released Emma's hand. "No. Whatever you do my love, please don't think, it's bad for us both when you do. Your brother and Abby both cut their wisdoms long ago and know their own business best. They won't thank you for interfering, and what's more, if you get me involved they'll blame it all on me, saying I should have stopped you."

"But it wouldn't be interfering, my love! I promise!"

"Don't try to bam me Emma, I know what you're about and I won't be part of it. You should heed my advice too, and not get involved."

Emma leant forward, throwing him the most imploring look she could manage. "Oh please my dearest, darling husband, it is such a little thing I need you to do – hardly interfering at all!"

But Alistair simply drained his brandy and set the glass down onto the side table with a loud thud. "No use looking at me like that my love, because I've said I won't get involved and there's not a dashed thing you can do to convince me otherwise."

CHAPTER FOUR

"Is Loughcroft feeling well?" Abigail asked her hostess the following day, "only he was rather quiet at the breakfast table. He seemed a touch distracted."

"Was he?" asked Emma in a serene voice as she worked on her embroidery. "I can't say that I noticed, but I have always found that men never are talkative before noon."

"No, perhaps I was mistaken," said Abigail with a shrug, and let the matter drop. "Are you sure that you don't need me to run any errands for you today? It would be no trouble for me."

Emma looked up. "Abby, you are here as my friend and my guest, not as an unpaid companion. If I need errands running I can do them myself. Or have Alistair run them for me."

Abigail shook her head, knowing better than to argue. "You are much too good to me, dearest, and I only hope I can be of use to you once your confinement begins."

Emma touched her stomach and smiled, "I am sure your godchild will keep you run off your feet from morning until night!"

"Is my sister planning your future for you, Mrs Merriweather? She will if you let her, you know," said George as he entered unannounced.

"My Lord!" exclaimed Abigail, half jumping out of her chair. Her hand went straight to her hair, as though she was checking that it was still as neat and stylish as always. Emma smiled to herself as she watched her friend's reaction.

"Ladies," said George with a graceful bow. "I have just received the oddest instruction from your husband, Emma. Not only has Loughcroft cancelled on a longstanding arrangement amongst a group of our peers, he seems to have excused me as well, then inexplicably vanished before I could challenge him over it."

"How strange," said Abigail, her face creasing up in a frown. "It is not at all like Loughcroft to do something so rag-mannered. I was only just saying to Emma that he did not seem quite himself this morning, almost as though he was preoccupied."

"It does seem a trifle out of character, doesn't it?" agreed George, but he was looking at Emma as he spoke. "He also left a note for me, requesting that I present myself here at my earliest convenience."

Emma set her embroidery aside with what she hoped was a dignified air. "I wonder at Alistair sometimes, he does get some peculiar starts, and I declare he did not indicate to me that he needed to speak to you urgently. He is not at home presently, but since you are here now there is something you could do to make yourself useful while you wait for him to return."

A smile threatened to dawn on George's lips, but he displayed enough sense and did not pursue this particular rabbit. "Ah, I suspected as much. What use can I be to you, my dearest sister?"

"You can teach Abby how to waltz."

"Teach me to waltz?" asked her friend in a shocked voice.

Emma turned to her, reaching out a hand. "Did you think I would not notice, dearest? For someone who loves dancing as much as you, I have never seen you stand up for a waltz, even when there have been several gentlemen requesting the honour. And I know full well that it is not because you regard the dance as too dashing; the only possible explanation is that you do not know the steps. For all my brother's faults he is a tolerable dancer, and I am sure that between us we can teach you."

"I know how to waltz, it's just that," she coloured up and stared at her hands. "Well the thing is that Mr Merriweather wasn't much for dancing, and then when he was sick it seemed quite inappropriate for me to be off enjoying myself while he was alone at home. And for all my reputation, I would not have dishonoured his memory by dancing while I was in mourning for him!"

"And so it has been a while since you had the opportunity to practice," finished George.

Abigail nodded with a relieved little sigh at his understanding. "I did try to hire a dancing instructor when Emma asked me to stay, but they were all booked up for the Season. I thought perhaps that I would be able to practice at some of the smaller gatherings, but when I realised that I was such a source of gossip for Lady Harden's set, nothing could induce me to make such a fool of myself in their presence."

"Of course you should not, which is why my scheme will answer perfectly. You can practice today with George, and then dance the waltz with him on Friday at the Putney ball."

"You have it all planned out, don't you, Sis?" said George, one eyebrow raised.

"I am sure that I have no idea what you could mean by that," replied Emma with a sniff. "But since events have conspired to lead us here, we might as well make the most of the situation."

Abigail and George shared a speaking look, but as neither of them raised an objection to her plan, Emma chose to ignore it. At her direction, they moved the chairs to the side of the room, giving them adequate space to dance.

"Do you want to watch us dance it first, dearest?" asked Emma, "to help remind you of the steps?"

"Only if she wants to learn how to dance like a walrus," said her brother. "You may dance well when you're not in the family way, Sis, but at this stage of your pregnancy you waddle far more than you walk."

"Well, of all the unjust things to say!" exclaimed Emma.

"Not unjust at all! I've had the dubious pleasure of watching your last few attempts at dancing, my dear girl, and the last thing Mrs Merriweather needs is to take lessons from you. In fact, I would be very grateful if you refrained from dancing in public until your child has put in an appearance – think of the family's reputation. Now be useful and play us a waltz on the pianoforte; I am sure that once we've had a few turns about the room it will all come back to Abigail."

Emma caught the glint of unholy amusement in her brother's eye, and with great difficulty bit down the pithy retort that flashed into her mind. "Abby dearest, if you would be so good as to partner with my brother, and forgive his ramshackle manners and oafish footwork, then we can commence with the practice."

"Just don't hit too many wrong notes," cautioned her brother, making Abigail giggle.

An excellent pianist, Emma played a basic waltz-air from memory as she watched her brother and best friend twirl about the room. At first Abigail held herself rigid in George's embrace. She frowned with concentration, but under George's excellent tutelage Abigail soon found her confidence. They spoke little and made even less eye contact, but Emma noted with satisfaction that her brother pulled Abigail closer to him than was strictly necessary for the Waltz, and that the widow was more than willing to let him. Gradually they relaxed, turning around the room in graceful movements, until they were holding each other's gaze and smiling.

Once again Emma was struck by how perfectly matched they were, and was gratified to see how beautifully they moved together. It was impossible to guess that Abigail had not waltzed for an age; in George's capable arms she moved as though she had been born to dance.

The piece of music came to an end and the couple parted, moving away with just enough reluctance to raise a silent cheer inside Emma's heart. There was hope for them both yet. She kept herself as still as possible, determined not to ruin the magic occurring between the dancers before her.

"Thank you, my Lord," said Abigail, her voice a touch faint. "I am sure that I will be able to waltz with tolerable ease at the Putney's ball."

"I would be honoured if you would accord me the pleasure of dancing a waltz with you," he replied with equal formality.

It was all Emma could do not to scream.

"Well the lesson went a touch better than I hoped," she said in a loud voice. "You did very well Abby dearest, but I regret to tell you that your footwork was slightly off."

Abigail gave a start at the sound of her voice, as though she had forgotten Emma was in the room. "Was it? I didn't realise. Oh dear, did I look very clumsy?"

"There was nothing wrong with her footwork," said George, his all-too-familiar frown darkening his face. "She danced very well."

"Yes, she did wonderfully when you consider that it has been so long since her last waltz," replied Emma as she stepped out from behind the pianoforte, "but I have a better view than you did, dear brother, and I am not about to let my friend out to dance under Old Bat Harden's gaze with her footwork less than perfect. I think perhaps we should try again, only I have some better sheet music in the other room. You two keep on practicing, I won't keep you above a few minutes, I promise."

If either her friend or her brother thought it odd that she should keep her sheet music in a separate room from that which housed the pianoforte, neither of them mentioned it. She closed the door behind her, feeling very pleased with herself and her subterfuge.

*

"Sisters," said George with real venom.

"Friends," muttered Abigail.

They looked at each and laughed. George felt the tension he had been carrying since the Hyde Park incident begin to melt away when she smiled at him.

"I wish to apologise for yesterday," he began, but she interrupted him before he could get any further.

"You have nothing to apologise for my Lord; indeed, you have apologised to me far too much already. I very much enjoyed our drive together, and you are in no way to blame for Lady Harden's dislike of me." The mischievous grin that both vexed and captivated him in equal measure peeped into existence. "Besides which, I think you have done sufficient penance for any crimes by having your planned entertainments cut short. Poor Loughcroft! What do you suppose Emma threatened to do in order to make him cancel on you in such a shabby manner?"

George shuddered. "That is not a subject that I wish to contemplate." He stepped towards her, holding out his hands. "I do, however, think we should heed my sister's advice and continue to practice the waltz. You may find it easier now you don't have to listen to that racket she calls music at the same time."

Abigail giggled, and was so much at ease as he slid his hands onto her waist he could not but yield to the temptation to pull her closer against him than was decent. Her mouth formed a little "o" of shock, but he began to lead her through the dance before she had the opportunity to pull away. He held her gaze as they moved, and wondered if it truly were possible for a man to drown in a pair of fine eyes.

"You dance very well, my Lord," whispered Abigail, and he felt an unfamiliar surge of triumph. For once he had succeeded in discomposing her in much the same way she did to him on a regular basis, and the experience was a sweet one.

"Call me George," he suggested. She hesitated, her gaze flitting from the floor to his eyes and back again. "Please," he added softly.

"As you wish," she said after another moment of silence. "You dance very well, George."

Hearing her say his name was everything he could have hoped for. Before he had a chance to think about the impropriety of his actions he had pulled her tight against him, and once he had done that there really was nothing left he could do but to kiss her.

She hesitated at first, but within a few moments her lips parted sufficiently to allow his tongue to slip into her mouth. She kissed him back with a passion that he had not expected - damn it all, he did not know what he had expected - but as her tongue collided with his it was all he could do not to crush her slim body against his. One of her hands was tangled into his hair, the other sliding down his back. He stopped thinking, and lost himself in the sensation of Abigail pressed against him.

*

Emma peeped her head around the door, then withdrew from the room before the occupants knew she was there. She glanced about to make sure there were no footmen present, and then performed a happy little jig in the hallway, congratulating herself on her matchmaking brilliance. After allowing a few minutes to pass, smug satisfaction at her own wisdom keeping her amused during her wait, she coughed loudly and opened the door to the sitting room.

"I have found the perfect piece of music for you to dance to – oh, I am glad that you have been practicing while I was out of the room, but really George, I hope you haven't been plaguing Abigail about her footwork; I swear I've never seen her so flustered before."

She busied herself at the pianoforte arranging her music sheets, chattering away as she ignored the irritated glare that her brother threw in her direction. Abigail said nothing, but her cheeks were a becoming shade of pink, and her fingers were pressed gently to her lips.

CHAPTER FIVE

There had been no occasion to talk after their kiss - although kiss hardly seemed an appropriate term for what had transpired between them. Emma had not left them alone after her return, even when Lord Loughcroft had eventually risked coming back home. Despite Emma's protestations that it would be no trouble at all to include him in their informal card party that evening, Lord Gloucester had declined the invitation and taken his leave, so that Abigail now found her thoughts on the matter quite confused.

He had kissed her. George Standing, the 4th Earl of Gloucester, the most starched-up, unbending high stickler she had ever met, had held her tight against him and *kissed her*. Just remembering the feel of his lips was enough to bring a blush to her cheeks and make her fingers creep up to her mouth, and she knew with certainty that had they not been interrupted, their passion would have gone further than a mere kiss. He was attracted to her and she to him, there was no denying that any longer, but for the life of her she could not work out his intentions.

She was subdued while dressing, so much so that her maid had to ask her three times whether she wanted to wear the shawl of Norwich silk that had pleased her so much when she purchased it at not a penny less than sixty guineas only the week before.

"Sorry, Martha, my thoughts were elsewhere. Yes, I will take the shawl, thank you. We should not be too late tonight, but do not wait up for me, I am quite capable of putting myself to bed, you know!"

Her maid looked scandalized by this suggestion. "Mr Merriweather would turn in his grave if he heard you! I gave him my solemn promise that I would take as good a care of you as if you were my own and I mean to keep by my word, make no mistake."

Abigail laughed and gave the older woman a quick hug. "You are too good to me," she said.

Martha sniffed, but her expression softened. "Well now, it's no more than my job to be, but you look fagged to death, if you don't mind me saying so. What you need is a good rest."

"Not at all, I just have a little headache. It is only a small gathering this evening, and I am sure that I will enjoy it immensely," said Abigail with perfect sincerity. When she had first seen the guest list it had been all she could do not to laugh; Emma had gone out of her way to invite only those persons who held Abigail in affection, or at the very least were too amiable to make her uncomfortable. By the time she left her room to rejoin her hostess, she was far enough in control of her emotions to present an

outward demeanour of serenity, no matter what was
going on in her heart.

It was a jolly gathering that assembled in Emma's
drawing room. Sir Joseph and Lady Putney were
amongst the first to arrive, and they set very little
store by formalities. Sir Joseph complimented Emma
on her growing form, shook Loughcroft's hand
vigorously and thanked him for the tip about the
sweet-goer newly purchased from an acquaintance,
and then pinched Abigail's chin, telling her she was
as beautiful as her mother but as wild as her father.

His wife shushed him, apologising for his poor
manners.

"It comes from his having been sent away to India
when he was young and getting into scrapes," she
told an amused Abigail with the same lack of care
that characterised her husband. "And I cannot be
but thankful for it. Lord alone knows what would
have become of him had he stayed in England and
carried on his rackety ways! He would have ended up
in Newgate, or dead from a duel no doubt, and then
what would have become of me? I would have been
married off to some prosy old bore, mark my words.
Now my dear girl, you simply must tell me where you
got that shawl, it is quite exquisite."

There was no opportunity to respond, for the rest
of Emma's guests began to arrive. In the round of
introductions and small talk that followed, there was
no chance for Abigail to chat with the one person

she most wished to converse. It was frustrating, but once the various games of cards began the chance finally presented itself.

Although a few of the gentlemen were playing vingt-et-un for pound stakes, the majority of the party were seated around the large card table, engrossed in a game of Silver Loo. Since Abigail was well known for her shocking lack of ability to grasp any form of cards, Lord Loughcroft had magnanimously offered to teach her the finer points of Piquet, even though it was obvious that the prospect very much lacerated his sensibilities. When Captain Rowlands declared that he had no luck at Loo, and was instead content to teach Abigail the differences between spades and clubs, Loughcroft surrendered his place at her side with unseemly haste, much to the amusement of the whole party.

"Fair Juno, how my days have been darkened without you," said Captain Rowlands as he took the seat opposite her at the small table. He shuffled the deck with the practised flair of a habitual gamer. "Lord Loughcroft was good enough to exchange places with me, for I declared to him that nothing could please me more than to witness the hands of a goddess as she played cards with me."

"Stop with the flummery Richard, there is no one here but me so you can drop this libertine act of yours," Abigail told him in an exasperated voice. "I need you to be serious for a moment!"

"Are you well, Abby? Has something happened?" asked the Captain, his brow creased with concern.

"Yes... No... Oh I don't know what I mean," mumbled Abigail as she watched him deal the cards out in front of her.

"Tell me all about it, dear heart. What are old friends for if they cannot help you to make sense of the world?"

Abigail, afraid that she would talk herself out of this course of action if she thought too much about it, decided to rush her fence. "What do they say about me, Richard? The Ton, I mean. Don't spare my feelings about it, I need you to be truthful. Emma and Alistair protect me, so I know it is bad."

He hesitated for a moment, his hand hovering over the cards before him. He met her gaze, then gave a small nod as if confirming something to himself. "Very well my dear. Your birth is impeccable as everyone knows; it is regarded as unfortunate that the daughter of a baron had to marry a merchant, but generally you are not held to fault at that. You have a reputation for being a trifle fast, and flying too close to the wind. No one would go so far as to call you a jade – well, perhaps Old Bat Harden, though she doesn't signify as everyone knows she has more spite than sense – but if you aren't careful, my dear, you are going to ruin yourself. As it stands, only the highest sticklers find anything offensive in your character, but somehow I doubt you will gain vouchers to Almacks anytime soon."

He spoke quietly so that no one else in the room could possibly have heard him, but the words hit Abigail with such force he may as well have shouted them. It was no worse than she had expected – perhaps even better than she had expected - but it hurt to hear it confirmed nonetheless.

"I see. Do you think then that there is any likelihood that a man of rank and breeding would have, well, would have honourable intentions by me?"

That got his attention. He put his hand of cards back down onto the table and gave her his full attention. "Has someone offered you a carte blanche, Abigail? Tell me his name and I'll call the damned impudent fellow out for the insult!"

Abigail was touched by his concern, but alarmed by his sincerity. "Well that would serve me an even worse trick, wouldn't it? Two men fighting over me, no doubt with pistols at dawn if I know you. Oh Lord, the scandal! You can come down off your high ropes, Richard, no one has offered me anything of the sort. It is just," she paused, her spirits lowering as confusion and doubt regained dominance in her thoughts. "It is just that someone has shown a decided preference for me, and I don't know what to make of it."

The soldier didn't answer straight away. He

regarded her with an uncharacteristic intensity and an unbecoming smirk playing across his lips. "My dear Mrs Merriweather, could it be that you lied to me? Is it possible that the Ice Goddess has gone and fallen in love?"

She snorted at that. "Don't be stupid, I've told you before that I'm not capable of such an emotion."

"Thou dost protest too much, fair Juno," he said as he picked his hand of cards back up. "Without knowing the precise nature of this decided preference as you call it, I don't think I could say with any certainty what this gentleman's intentions are by you. However," he said, cutting her off as she began to interrupt him, "if it is who I believe that it is, then I would be surprised to learn that the fellow is capable of being anything but honourable in his intentions. Nothing against the man, but seems a bit dull that way."

Abigail felt her heart beat a little faster. Captain Rowlands seemed aware of her inner turmoil, and changed the subject. He began to run through the rules of piquet, reminding her of all the occasions her late husband had laughingly scolded her for her lack of interest in cards. The memories of those good times did much to restore her good humour, and if her heart ached a little at the loss of a man whom she had held in a great deal of affection, laughing with Richard over the time she got clubs and spades confused, or the time she accidentally won a whole litter of pugs from the Misses Clark, put her much more at ease.

"So, do you think that maybe you like London today?" asked the Captain once Abigail had fully regained her composure.

"I think so," she said after a moment's consideration, "although I can't help but think that life would have been easier if I had stayed in Yorkshire." She turned to look at the noisy game of Loo behind her and smiled. "And sometimes I think I need reminding that I do have friends here in the city as well."

"I was a touch surprised that the Hardens were not here this evening."

Abigail gave a theatrical shudder. "How awful if they had been invited!"

"I'll grant you that about the old bat, but Miss Harden could not be considered contemptible," said the Captain.

Abigail considered that for a moment. "No, I suppose not, although I have barely exchanged ten words with her, since her mother thinks I am an improper person to strike a friendship with her daughter. Poor Charlotte. She'd look a lot better if the Old Bat didn't keep putting her in the most unbecoming outfits, don't you agree? Come to think of it, she'd be better off away from Lady Harden all together."

"I heard that her grandmother had offered to take Miss Harden into her care, but the Old Bat refused."

"Did Emma tell you about that? How unlike her to discuss her family - but then I think she is half in love with your scarlet coat."

"Then I count my blessings that she is quite obviously head over heels in love with her husband."

Abigail laughed. "They are terribly unfashionable about it, aren't they? It is part of why I like them so much. Did you know that it was her Aunt Seraphinia who promoted the match between them? She is quite a formidable woman, but she would not countenance her relatives marrying for less than love - in fact she insisted upon it. I believe that even Gloucester is a little in awe of the woman. I met her a few times back in my schoolroom days; kind, but I was terrified the whole time."

"She sounds like a dragon."

"She is, but only in the best possible way! Emma says that she hates Lady Harden with a passion, and that they have barely spoken since Lord Harden died. It is such a pity, because I think her influence would do Charlotte a whole world of good." She grinned as a thought struck her. "How I would love to see the dragon pitted against the Old Bat! I know who my money would be on!"

"Indeed," said Richard, but he seemed bored by the gossip. He motioned to the hand of cards lying before her, yet to be picked up. "Talking of putting money down, shall we play?"

It was an enjoyable game, and even if it was painfully obvious to her that Richard let her win several hands, he did so with such flair that she was unable to call him on it. They gave up cards and instead moved to join the small group enjoying a comfortable chat around the fireplace.

"Dear, dear Mrs Merriweather, I was just telling Mr Ramsgate here all about your adventure at the balloon ascension!" said Lady Putney with jovial enthusiasm.

Abigail didn't know whether to laugh or cry at this disclosure. "My Lady please do not! I have promised the Loughcrofts that I will not do anything so scandalous again; I doubt my reputation would survive it."

"Stuff and nonsense!" said Lady Putney. "You might as well ask the tide not to come in. You, my dear girl, are what Sir Joseph calls pluck to the backbone. You can't help but get into scrapes, and a jolly good thing it is, too! Girls these days are far too simpering for my tastes."

"I am hardly a girl, but I thank you for implying I am younger than my years, and I promise you that the incident at the balloon ascension had nothing to do with pluck! Had I even *suspected* that those boys would loosen the ropes the way they did…"

"Then you would have missed out on a great adventure, which you very much enjoyed," said Lady Putney, crossing her plump arms. "You can't fool me with these airs of yours, Mrs Merriweather – and I tell you now that they don't suit! Do not let the vulgar tittle-tattle of a few jealous old matrons lead you to hide your light. Sir Joseph finds you refreshing, as do I, so for every high stickler you've upset, there are at least two members of the ton who like you for it!"

Abigail was much moved by this. "Thank you, that is very kind of you to say."

"Nothing of the sort," sniffed Lady Putney. "I have always believed in speaking as I find things, so there you go. I very much look forward to seeing you at my ball, and I trust that you will be back to your usual form by then."

"Then I promise you faithfully that I shall not disappoint you, my Lady!" said Abigail, pointedly ignoring the little groan of concern uttered by Captain Rowlands.

CHAPTER SIX

Friday arrived, but there had been no visit from Lord Gloucester. Alistair provided some vague intelligence to the effect that the Earl had been called out of town on short notice, but Abigail could not help but feel that he should at the very least have sent a card or note to her.

With a real effort, she tried to convince herself that she was grateful he had gone away and was thus saved from the embarrassment of seeing him again, but failed miserably. She missed him, but whether she blamed Lord Gloucester or herself for this state of affairs depended very much on the direction of the wind at any given moment.

She busied herself in the morning by riding through the park on the pretty mare Lady Loughcroft had brought to London for her to use, silently thanking her friend for her thoughtfulness. Although the morning was crisp and the exercise welcome, it did little to relieve the melancholy that had been creeping over her ever since the card party.

Emma had forced her to practice waltzing again, this time with Alistair as her partner, and although the Viscount danced with impeccable grace, holding her at the correct distance and making her laugh with his droll observations, it had not felt right to have his hands about her waist. She had found herself longing to be held once again by the Earl.

This simply would not do.

Abigail had long despised those simpering misses who would go into a decline when the man they had set their heart on showed no inclination to return their regard. It seemed such a stupid waste of effort, and never one that would result in the gentleman in question falling head over ears in love with the damsel. By the time she had returned to Berkeley Square she had decided that the best thing to do was attend the Putney Ball in her best looks and leave the whole Ton in no doubt that she was happy and comfortable in her current circumstances, and to that end had decided on the precise outfit to wear.

In a somewhat better mood that she had been when she left for her ride, Abigail entered the Loughcroft's mansion humming a waltz. She skipped up the stairs to her room with the intention of seeking Martha's opinion with regards to her hair, and whether that good lady thought her new slippers would complement the dress she had in mind for the ball.

As she opened the door she stopped in surprise as the sheer number of bouquets piled on every available surface reducing her to stunned silence. Cascades of roses in every imaginable hue flowed across the dressing table and her bed stand, the air filled with their strong, sweet aroma.

"Oh, Mrs Merriweather!" exclaimed her maid, who was stood in the middle of the room surrounded by flowers. "I swear I have never seen so many beautiful blooms at once!"

Emma, who was seated on Abigail's bed, agreed with her. "Indeed, someone has gone to a lot of trouble to make sure that the flowers you wear to the ball tonight were the ones they sent you."

"These... these are all from one person?" asked Abigail in a faint voice. She leant down to touch the petals of a pretty yellow rose, delighting in the smoothness beneath her fingertips.

"Yes, the ones from your other admirers are in the drawing room," replied Emma. "We could not fit them all in here."

"Who sent them?"

Emma pointed at the dressing table. "The card is over there, dearest."

Abigail opened the card with trembling fingers, not quite sure why her heart was beating so fast. The message, written out in the Earl's beautiful hand, made her head whirl.

My Dearest Abigail,

Despite scouring the hothouses and gardens at every one of my estates, I could not find a bloom that compares to you. Please do me the honour of wearing some of these paltry offerings to the ball tonight, and save the waltz for me.

Ever yours,

George.

Emma gave a loud cough as she stood up, recalling Abigail to the present. "I shall leave you to change, my dear. All of a sudden I feel the urge to tell my husband of this romantic gesture being shown to my best of friends. I may sigh a lot and look heartbroken while I do so, although it will probably have little effect." She paused at the bedroom door, turning to look at Abby with a decided twinkle in her eye. "I do look forward to the day our relationship is closer than just friends," she said, leaving the room before Abigail had a chance to respond.

*

Any ball or gathering held by the Putneys was guaranteed to be well attended. Lady Putney was an exemplary hostess with an exquisite eye for detail and an innate talent to put everyone at their ease. Although some of the highest sticklers may deplore her lack of exclusivity or her husband's devil-may-care approach to society, even those top-lofty few would not turn down an invitation to their ball, which almost always proved to be a highlight of the Season. It helped that their three sons were all amiable, good looking, and each set to inherit enough money to buy a small country. There was not a matchmaking mama in England who did not have their eye on one of those young men, so it was inevitable, really, that the Putney's ball would always be something of a squeeze.

When they entered the ballroom, Abigail had the pleasure of knowing that her outfit had caused several heads to turn and drawn many admiring glances. She had briefly flirted with the idea of wearing her beautiful, if unremarkable, ivory gown of spangle lace, but the desire to cut a dash had won out over the urge to appear respectable. Abigail reconciling herself with the reflection that the last time she had worn such an outfit to a society ball the Earl had been unable to keep his eyes off her all night.

Her silk dress of Pomona green drew as many envious stares at it did disproving ones. Although the design was simplicity itself, the hem was cut as high as decency allowed, while the neckline was as daring as Society would permit. A strict follower of Beau Brummell's teachings, she had assured herself that she had not a hair out of place before leaving her bedchamber, and now gave no outward indication that she was conscious of her appearance.

Inside, however, was a different story altogether, and it took great effort not to smooth down her dress or glance at her reflection in the hall mirrors. She silently prayed that no one would guess just how obsessed she was with appearing to advantage this evening.

It seemed like half of London had turned out, and a generous splash of scarlet coats showed that many of the Army's finest were in attendance. The most fashionable ladies present counted at least one officer amongst their court, and those women lucky enough to have two, or even three soldiers dance attendance upon her drew envious glances from those who could only dream of such conquests.

The Loughcrofts were stopped and greeted by several friends, but thanks in part to Emma's sizeable stomach they found some chairs easily enough from where they could easily observe the other guests. Abigail was proud enough not to openly scan the crowds for Lord Gloucester's presence, but under the cover of pointing out acquaintances to Emma, she was able to search for him.

She had pinned some of the roses he had sent to her dress, delicate cream blooms that had a delicious scent about them. A nagging voice at the back of her mind kept insisting that she was mistaken about his feelings, that marriage was the last thing the Earl desired from a trade widow and that her actions were foolish.

A half hour passed with surprising speed, and although Abigail was tolerably certain that none of the various acquaintances who stopped to chat were aware of her inner turmoil, her closest friend lay in no doubt of the truth.

"Don't worry, Abby; he will be here to dance with you," said Emma with a smile.

She was about to throw a sarcastic rejoinder at Emma, designed to leave her friend in no doubt about the fact she had completely forgotten the Earl's promise to waltz with her, when a depreciative cough captured her attention, and she turned to see Lord Gloucester make a flourishing bow.

There was no other way to describe him; he was complete to a shade. Resplendent in full evening dress, his coat of blue superfine seemed to be moulded across his well-formed shoulders, and his neckcloth – arranged to perfection in the Trone D'Amour – was a thing of beauty. Although he was far from the most elaborately dressed man there, he was certainly the most commanding.

"I owe you an apology, Mrs Merriweather," he said.

Abigail frowned; of everything she had expected him to say, "sorry" had never occurred to her. He seemed to be making a habit of apologising to her. "What for, my Lord?"

"For daring to send you such insipid flowers as these roses. I thought them to be beautiful, but now that I see you wearing them I realise that I was quite wrong."

She felt her cheeks warm in response to his gallantry, and held out her hand to him. "You'll turn my head with such flattery, my Lord. Quick, condemn me for something and all will be right with the world."

That drew a laugh, but he did not avail himself of her invitation. Instead, he settled for kissing her fingertips and keeping hold of her hand for as long as decency allowed. Abigail's heart thundered, drowning out all the noise of the ball as she thought, for just one incredible moment, that he was going to throw propriety to the wind and kiss her again.

Someone gave a little cough from beside her. Emma, or perhaps Alistair. It didn't matter, for the Earl blinked a few times, as if suddenly recalled to his location, and let go of her hand with a rueful smile.

He exchanged pleasantries with his sister, and greeted Alistair with a disparaging remark about his neckcloth. Abigail gave herself a little shake, reminded herself of her surroundings, then followed his lead and joined in the conversation.

They spent a comfortable few minutes sharing the latest on-dits of London, and Emma secured her brother's word that he would attend a small picnic that she was holding the following week. While Emma turned to inform her husband of this considerable social triumph, the Earl leant over towards Abigail, his voice quiet so as to keep their conversation private.

"There is something of a very personal nature I wish to ask you, my dear Abigail, but this is sadly not the occasion. Will you forgive my impertinence and grant me a private interview tomorrow?"

Her heart began to thunder again as the world stilled around her. She nodded weakly, not quite trusting herself to speak.

He covered her hand with his and gave it a little squeeze. "Thank you. What time will suit you best?"

"Gloucester, there you are!" Lady Harden's foghorn voice interrupted them before Abigail could answer. A look of sheer exasperation flashed across the Earl's face, and he let go of her hand again. She was surprised at how lost that made her feel.

"Cousin," said the Earl as Lady Harden descended upon them, towing her meek daughter along in her wake. "How do you do?"

"Quite exhausted after having to search you out in these crowds. Really, this house is most inconveniently laid out for a ball. I am surprised that Lady Putney would invite more people than she can comfortably fit into her rooms."

"No, but I hear that the Prince was unwilling to lend her the Palace for her ball, on account that it might outshine his own affair," said Gloucester. Abigail turned away so that Lady Harden could not see her laughter.

"Well, be that as it may, it has been quite difficult to find you in these crowds!"

"I am sorry to hear that you put yourself to so much trouble, but I have not got the faintest notion as to why you would wish to seek me out."

Lady Harden gave a neigh of a laugh, as false as the elaborate arrangement of fruit that topped her large puce turban. "Wretch! You are famed for your lamentable memory, but even you could not forget your promise to dance with my dearest Charlotte in the Cotillion! They are forming up in the next room, and if you are quick you will not miss it."

From the look on Gloucester's face, Abigail got the impression that he had never promised to dance with Miss Harden, and was about to tell his cousin just that. However inopportune a moment Lady Harden had picked to descend upon them, Abigail could not bring herself to blame Charlotte, who was staring at the floor as though she wished it would swallow her whole.

"Gloucester, how could you?" said Abigail, tapping his wrist with her fan. The Earl looked at her, somewhat confused. "You were so wrapped up in telling me about your horses that you must have been unaware of the dancing! I am sure that Miss Harden will forgive you, and perhaps even still dance with you if you ask her prettily enough."

He didn't respond straight away, but a quick

glance from her face to Charlotte's seemed to soften him. He bowed to the poor girl, extending his arm. "Your servant, Miss Harden! I promised you a dance and hope you will forgive my lamentable memory. Old age, you know, can creep up on a man at any time."

"Can it really, sir?" asked Charlotte as she accepted the proffered arm.

"Indeed it can," said Gloucester as he led her off to the dance, "it has even been known to shown signs of development in the schoolroom."

Abigail watched them go, just about managing to smother her laughter. Lady Harden was not fooled, and with a little *"Humph!"* of disapproval, flounced off in search of better company.

Emma sent off Alistair in search of refreshments, and the two friends settled down to the enjoyable task of analysing the outfits of every lady present at the ball. They had only a few minutes to indulge themselves before a flood of scarlet coats surrounded them, demanding their attention.

"Lady Loughcroft, your most humble servant! Have you been left without an escort? This will not do! Allow me to stand your champion!"

Emma gave an appreciative giggle and stretched out her hand as Captain Rowlands, his behaviour as audacious as ever, brushed his lips to her fingertips. He let her hand drop and turned to face Abigail, feigning surprise at finding her sat beside Lady Loughcroft.

"Why there you are, my fairest Juno, I have been searching for you this past hour! You commanded me to show my presence, and here I am. Sadly I could not shake off my brother officers, who demanded that I introduce them to the scandalous Mrs Merriweather. I pray, oh queen of all goddesses, that you will forgive me for bringing such meagre specimens to your attention."

Abigail rolled her eyes. "You get more absurd every time we meet," she told him in a disapproving tone, knowing full well he would ignore her attempts to scold him. "And please do not go around calling me scandalous! I am nothing of the sort!"

"But that is not true, Mrs Merriweather," said a young officer with a cheeky smile. "When I discovered that Rowly here was an old friend of the lady who flew in a hot air balloon over the palace a mere week before racing down St James' in a high perch phaeton, what could I do but beg him to introduce me to you?"

Captain Rowlands interrupted as Abigail grew hot with embarrassment. "Lady Loughcroft, Mrs Merriweather, allow me to introduce you to my fellow officers; Percy, Dawlish and Bingham. Rapscallions to a man, and all eternally grateful that they look well in a military coat!"

The introductions were made, the soldiers each bowing to the ladies with elegance. Dawlish, the soldier who had joked with her about the balloon incident, begged pardon so prettily that she forgave him for bringing it up, and then laughed as the youngest and most junior of the officers, Ensign Percy, asked if she remembered him.

"Indeed I do remember you, although you were still Master Charles Percy then! Would you believe, Lady Loughcroft, that my late husband once caught this fellow trying to climb up one of our apple trees for a dare? Why, that feels like only yesterday!"

"He boxed my ears roundly for that, but Mrs Merriweather took pity on me, and gave me a slice of apple pie to help heal my bruised ego," said Percy with a cheerful grin. He turned to Abigail and bowed. "May I beg the honour dancing with you this evening, by way of apology for my youthful misdemeanours?"

"I am afraid that I have promised my next few dances already, but I am sure that I can save a country dance for you!"

"Only if you will dance with me too, Mrs Merriweather," said Lieutenant Bingham. "You cannot dance with Percy only to deny Dawlish and me the same honour!"

She consulted her dance card and then shook her head.

"But I am afraid that I have only one free dance remaining, so I can partner with only one of you fine military men, or none at all."

Good natured banter ensued at this comment, with each of the soldiers loudly demanding that they should be afforded the opportunity to dance with Abigail. As Captain Rowlands had already bespoken Abigail's hand for the quadrille, he was considered ineligible for the competition. Before long they were all addressing their pleas to Emma, who laughed and encouraged their banter with an appreciative gleam in her eyes.

"Lady Loughcroft, I beseech you to convince Mrs Merriweather that she should partner with me, for I am by far the best dancer in the regiment!" said Major Dawlish.

"Perhaps, but you are by far the ugliest too," said Captain Rowlands to the laughter of the other men.

"Percy cannot be considered eligible, for he is well known to confuse his left and right when trying to march. As a fellow officer I could not let him embarrass himself in front of such esteemed company," said Bingham.

"So tragic that Lieutenant Bingham fell from his horse only yesterday," said young Percy with a sigh, "he has complained all day that his leg is stiff as result of his misfortune, and must now count himself out of this competition."

"Not at all," announced the Lieutenant. "Being in the presence of two such exquisite ladies has miraculously cured me."

So the conversation continued with Abigail encouraging each of them equally, until Emma finally decreed that Major Dawlish, by virtue of not scoring any points against his fellow officers and instead relying on his own merits to prove himself worthy, had won the right to dance with Abigail. Her announcement was met with good natured complaints and promises of pistols at dawn before the soldiers took their leave of them.

"Did you see that? It is not enough for her to wear the most improper clothing — for nothing will convince me that her skirts cling like that without being dampened — but then she must flirt openly with an entire regiment!"

The angry little voice reached Abigail's ears, and she felt stomach tighten. Out the corner of her eye she saw two unmarried women of indeterminate age staring at her, not even trying to disguise their gossiping. Her anger began to bubble up, but before she could respond Emma placed a cool hand over hers and gave her head an infinitesimal shake.

"Did you hear that she strode down St James Street unescorted, and tried to enter one of the gentlemen's clubs? It must be true, because my Aunt Elinor told me, and she is close friends with Lady Harden, you know."

Emma squeezed her hand tighter.

"It would not surprise me at all. Her late husband was a tradesman which accounts for her lack of gentility. I have often heard that those who marry beneath their social standing lose something of their bronze as a result. Tragic, but she is living proof of it. I for one would not be so vulgar as to try and keep four soldiers dangling in my pocket for a full half hour!"

This was too much for Abigail. She pulled her hand free from Emma's and twisted around to face the two women. "That is very fortunate, for any attempt on your part to do so would only end in embarrassment for all concerned."

The woman gave a gasp of shock. "I have never been spoken to in such a way before!"

"Haven't you?" asked Abigail in a bored voice. "Having overheard your conversation, you do surprise me."

"Abigail, that is enough," said Emma in an urgent murmur. Abigail might have left it at that, but the woman's friend puffed up like an offended pigeon as she tried to recover lost ground.

"If by that you mean we dislike seeing a Female behaving in such a low manner with rakes in uniform, then-"

Abigail did not give her the chance to finish.

"What I mean is that a pair of cattish ape-leaders are not fit to comment on such matters, and that those who deal in such gossip must have very dull lives. I pity you both, and ask that you keep your jealous observations to yourself. If I wish to encourage soldiers to hang about me then that is my decision, for it would take no more than a snap of my fingers and I can have any tradesman, soldier or nobleman I choose dance attendance on me, from a lowly ensign up to an Earl!"

The moan of dismay from Emma let her know that she had once again crossed the line of good behaviour. Abigail spun around to see Gloucester, his face white and his eyes as hard as glass, standing only a few feet away from her. He said nothing. He did not even acknowledge that she had spoken. Before her mind could form the words to apologise, to explain, to say anything; he gave a stiff bow and continued walking until he disappeared into the next room.

"I think you may be aiming too high," said the smug woman behind her. Her companion tittered.

Abigail was proud of herself for not causing another scandal by throwing her drink over them, but doubted that anyone else would appreciate her restraint.

CHAPTER SEVEN

George danced the next set with the young daughter of an old friend; a pretty enough child of seventeen, but she was shy and rarely answered his questions with more than a frightened "*yes, sir,*" or "*no, my Lord.*"

The set lasted a full half hour, and throughout that time he was treated to tantalising glimpses of Abigail Merriweather as she danced with a tall, handsome soldier. She moved with all her usual grace, her eyes were bright and her laughter only served to enhance her beauty.

George was thankful when the dancing finally came to an end and he could escort his young companion back to her waiting mother. He spied Alistair Loughcroft and a group of friends on the far side of the room, and made his way over to them. He made idle small talk for a short while, but his eyes were on Abigail as she crossed the room on the arm of another dashing blade in a military uniform. A stab of jealousy cut right through to his heart, and he turned away so that he could not see her laughing.

Lord Loughcroft moved to stand beside him.

"You were stupid, you know," said Alistair. "You made Abby look foolish."

"She did that herself," replied George, but without conviction. Guilt over his own conduct had long since drowned his anger.

"No it was definitely you, old fellow. Abby was winning that battle with the old tabbies until you showed up. I'd have thought that you would know by now that she has a dashed quick tongue in her head. Would you rather she had sat there all prim and proper while she could hear her nature, her birth, her late husband and her intellect called into disrepute? Doing it too brown, George! Far too brown!"

The truth of this observation cut to the quick. Despite Alistair's conversational tone, George felt like he'd received a rake down at the hands of a master.

"She shouldn't have said it, of course," continued his friend, "but I'll be damned if I would have thought more of her for behaving with propriety. Not at all the thing, what those women said about her, and I was impressed by her retort. Thing is, Abby is full of pluck and that's what I like about her, and despite your claims to the contrary, I rather thought it was what you liked so much about her, too."

He did not wait for an answer, instead sauntering off towards Lord Putney as though he had been talking of nothing but everyday trivialities.

The next dancing set was beginning to form, and

Abigail was led to the floor by a handsome young Marquis whose mother would no doubt be terrified about the prospect of him falling in love with the scandalous Mrs Merriweather. The image made him smile, and he admitted to himself that, no matter how many of the Ton's matchmaking mamas took Abigail in dislike, she would always be popular amongst the dashing, the fun-loving and the gentlemen. As he watched her walk to her position on the dance floor, somehow managing to take the shine out of every other damsel present without effort, he realised that he would not have her any other way.

As if conscious of being watched, Abigail turned her head and locked eyes with him. She raised her chin just a fraction, a defiant gesture that made him smile before he could help himself. He bowed, and then winked. He had the satisfaction of seeing shock register on the widow's face for a split second before laughter replaced it. She threw a saucy wink back and then turned away, her full attention returning to her dance partner.

George walked away, planning to amuse himself at the card table until the dance finished and he would be at leisure to once again apologise to Abigail – an occurrence that was becoming something of a habit with him, he realised with a grin.

He caught sight of Miss Harden lurking at the edge of the corridor and, suspecting that her mother would be close by, was about to walk in the opposite direction, when something about her body language made him pause.

She stood in the entrance of a small alcove and seemed to be in great distress as she shook her head vigorously, her dull brown ringlets bouncing about her face like weak springs. It appeared that someone was holding tight to her wrist to prevent her from running away.

"May I be of service, Miss Harden?"

Charlotte gave out a little squeak of surprise. "My Lord Gloucester! No I am... that is to say... I am quite... oh, oh dear!" her grey eyes filled with tears as she looked around her for an escape route.

"Good evening, Lord Gloucester," said a male voice. Captain Rowlands stepped out of the alcove, his face grim. George felt all of his dislike for the soldier rise up once again as he surmised the nature of what he had stumbled upon. Charlotte was not the greatest of heiresses on the market, but her fortune was not to be sniffed at – certainly not by a penniless rake out to snag a rich wife.

"You should take your leave now, Captain Rowlands," said George.

The soldier puffed up, anger flaring across his face. "You have interrupted a private conversation between Miss Harden and myself, sir."

George offered his arm to Charlotte, who took it

in meek silence. Her head was bowed down and she did not acknowledge either of them. "I do not know what type of conversation I interrupted, Captain Rowlands, but Miss Harden does not appear keen to continue it. I suggest you go search for entertainment elsewhere."

For a moment, George wondered if the soldier would lose his temper and attempt to start a brawl. He knew full well the scale of the scandal such a set-to would cause, but by God, for one moment he actually wanted the man to swing at him.

Despite his obvious inner struggle, Captain Rowlands did not do anything so ill bred. He stared at Charlotte for a moment, his eyes almost pleading. "Forgive me, Miss Harden," he said, before giving a stiff bow and walking off.

"Are you well, child?" George asked Charlotte in a gentle voice.

"Yes sir, thank you."

"Do you wish to return to your mother?" He almost smiled at the look of horror that flashed across her face. "Silly question. How about we fetch something to drink, and find somewhere to watch the dancing?"

Charlotte gave a sigh of relief. "Thank you, sir, I am very much obliged."

George shook his head as they walked, suddenly

feeling very old.

*

The dance ended, and the young Marquis grudgingly gave up Abigail into the company of Lady Loughcroft. Emma had pleaded her pregnancy as an excuse for not joining in any of the dance sets, and Abigail rather suspected that Lord Gloucester's cutting comments about his sister's propensity to waddle rather than walk had struck home. Despite this, Emma appeared to be enjoying herself immensely. She had gathered a court made up of gallant gentlemen who were happy to flirt and entertain, but knew exactly where to draw the line. Her husband spent more time with her than was fashionable, and many of his friends came to pay her their respects.

"Abigail, you simply have to listen to the story Mr Greenman has been telling me, so droll!"

Abigail made a polite curtsey and took the seat proffered by one of her friend's admirers. She accepted their laughing banter about her exploits, blushed as they recounted the more scandalous moments, and promised several that she had not forgotten she was pledged to dance with them later in the evening.

"Are you calmer now, dearest?" asked Emma at the earliest opportunity.

"I think so," she replied. She thought about the

way the Earl had looked at her before he had been audacious enough to wink. "In fact, I would say yes, I am much calmer."

"And happier," said Emma with a satisfied nod. "That is good. It would break Lady Putney's heart to know that even a single one of her guests was unhappy. She prides herself on throwing some of the best parties in London, and insists that we all enjoy them."

"Then we had better not tell her that you were complaining of swollen ankles and are unable to dance," retorted Abigail. "Really dearest, how thoughtless of you to get in the family way when you knew that you would have to attend Lady Putney's ball this year."

"I am a selfish creature, aren't I? I shall just have to — good grief, is that Miss Harden with my brother?"

On the far side of the room the Earl was sat beside Charlotte, at obvious pains to engage the girl. As she was a shy thing at the best of times, this appeared to be taxing Gloucester's ingenuity to the limit. Although Miss Harden spent more time looking at her hands than anywhere else, she occasionally glanced up at his face for a brief moment, and once even rewarded him with a smile.

"Looks like it," said Abigail, "although how the poor thing has managed to shake her mother off for a few minutes, I can't tell. I didn't think it was possible."

"Most likely because she is sitting with my brother," muttered Emma. "My relative is hardly discreet in her attempts to throw the two of them together at every turn. I think it is a big part of her dislike for you, dearest!"

"Which proves she's a silly goose. Does she really have her eye on Gloucester as a son-in-law?"

"Undoubtedly, but only because none of the Dukes show a preference for Charlotte's company."

"But neither does Gloucester," pointed out Abigail.

"True, but he is forced to acknowledge the Hardens due to our family connection, so she is easily able to convince herself that Charlotte is growing in his heart."

"Poor girl, with a mother like that it's no wonder that she's still on the shelf at twenty-one. I mean, she's a pretty enough thing – at least, she would be if she stopped dressing her in that hideous shade of pink – but who on earth could stomach Lady Harden for their mother-in-law?"

"I think it is more a case of who could Lady Harden stomach as a son-in-law. She's always been full of her own self importance – that's half the reason she fell out with my Aunt Seraphinia! - and will accept nothing less than a Viscount for her daughter."

Abigail shook her head. "Poor thing hasn't got a chance."

"No," said Emma with a frown. "Do you know, perhaps I should write to my Aunt, advise her to invite Charlotte to stay for a while. Lady Harden won't like it, but it might do Charlotte some good to be under her grandmother's care for a while."

Captain Rowlands approached and brought their conversation to a close. "Fair Juno, you promised a waltz to me, and I am here to collect."

Abigail frowned. The Captain's tone was somehow mocking, and although he gave no outward signs of inebriation, the thought that he might be drunk crossed her mind. She dismissed it. In all the years she had known him he had never once treated a woman with disrespect, and she was yet to understand where his reputation as a rake had come from. She accepted his hand and let him lead her to the dance floor. A quick glance told her that Gloucester was still engaged with Miss Harden, and the rueful smile he threw towards her warmed her heart.

The music began. Abigail placed her hands onto the Captain's shoulders as he slipped his hands onto her waist. There was nothing amorous in his hold, and although the mocking look remained on his face, he did not say anything to make her uncomfortable.

"Do you remember, Abby, when you told me that all I need do is ask should I require your help?"

"Yes, and I meant it. You have been a good friend to me, Richard."

"I've made a real hum of my affairs, Abby, and I don't know if I can come about. At least I'm a soldier; if the enemy don't kill me, I suppose I could blow my brains out instead."

Abby's eyes widened in alarm. "Very likely you could, but I'm sure things are not as desperate as that."

"Oh, it is. My enemies have put it about that I am a penniless rake, and now my prospects are ruined." He glared over her shoulder and across the room. As the dance moved them around Abigail followed his gaze until she came to see Lord Gloucester and Charlotte Harden seated at the edge of the dance floor, with the Old Bat bearing down on them.

"Lady Harden," she muttered.

"Amongst others."

"We'll she's managed to upset Gloucester again, he's gone rigid. Oh, and poor Charlotte! She's just practically fled from the room."

"Where?" asked the Captain, turning to look. The

movement caused him to miss a step, much to Abigail's annoyance.

"Richard, you're throwing out my timings."

Recalled to his location, the Captain returned his full attention to her. "Sorry, Abby. It is just that – oh blast this dance. I need to talk to you."

"Well don't think that we're running off before the music finishes, Richard Rowlands. It was you who pointed out that my reputation was edging towards the scandalous, so you can at least do me the favour of getting through this dance with a touch of grace!"

Her comment raised a smile from him, but it did not reach his eyes. She spent the rest of the waltz doing her best to soothe his temper, well aware that several pairs of gossip-hungry eyes were watching them. She could hear it already; a lover's quarrel, perhaps, or maybe she would be accused of finally demanding marriage from the rakish soldier.

She was suddenly so very tired, and wanted to be out of their gaze. The uncomfortable truth was that, no matter what happened in her future, there would always be a portion of the Ton who refused to accept her back into their number.

The music ended. Abby looked back to where she had last seen Gloucester, but he was gone. A quick glance at Emma reassured her that her friend had more than enough admirers to look after her, and she would not be needed for a while.

"Let us find somewhere private to talk," she said in a low voice. "Then you can tell me what you need from me."

Captain Rowlands led her away from the crowded ballroom. They stepped through into an unlit room that, in the darkness, Abigail guessed might be a small sitting room for the Putney's. Richard worked his way over to the windows and pulled back the large, heavy curtains, bathing the room in moonlight so bright it was as if he had lit a dozen candles.

A little gasp came from behind them. Abigail jumped back as a small, muslin-clad figure threw herself into the soldier's arms. "Richard, oh Richard, it is all at an end and there is no hope!"

Abigail blinked a few times, her gaze flitting between that of the Captain as he cooed soothing nothings, and the somewhat crumpled and tearstained Charlotte Harden, who was crushing his jacket in quite a worrying fashion.

"Hush now, my darling, we will come about!" said Captain Rowlands, but Charlotte shook her head vigorously.

"Oh if only I had listened to you, and not gone with Lord Gloucester. I am sorry I quarreled quarrelled with you my darling, I was just so unhappy, and now it is all at an end!"

Abigail stared at them, trying to make sense of their tangled conversation, and failing. "Would someone like to tell me what is going on?" she asked. Miss Harden gave a squeak of fear, as though she had only just noticed a third person in the room.

Captain Rowlands kissed Charlotte on the top of her head.

"Hush there, dearest. Mrs Merriweather will stand our friend." He smiled at Abigail, but the lines around his eyes were tight. "Are you shocked, fair Juno? Charlotte and I are in love, and I very much wish to marry her."

"Oh and I want to marry you, my darling, but we must not torture ourselves like this. There is no hope!" cried Charlotte, staring up into his face with all the innocent adoration of a kitten.

This melodramatic outburst served more to puzzle Abigail than to alarm her. "I always find that hope tends to hide in the most unexpected of places, Miss Harden. Now, I collect that this is the problem that Richard wanted my help to solve, so why don't you tell me the whole and see if between us we can't come up with something?"

Charlotte turned to Abigail, her eyes wide with fear. Not for the first time Abigail wondered how there could only be six years between them in age; Charlotte seemed absurdly young. "There is nothing anyone can do. Mama has told me that the Earl is going to offer for me, and that I must accept. I have never been so unhappy in all my life!"

It was a good thing that this announcement ended on a sob, and that Charlotte felt compelled to bury her face once again into the Captain's jacket. She did not see the look of shock, swiftly followed by unholy amusement, which passed between her dearest love and Abby.

"Which Earl in particular, my love? There are several of them."

"Lord Gloucester," she replied in a trembling voice. "I swear I had no notion of it, Richard, and thought that he was only being nice to me, after seeing us quarrel earlier. Only Mama said that everyone was talking about it for he stayed by my side for an improper length of time, and that he has singled me out for attention on so many occasions. The whole of the Ton is expecting him to make me an offer, Mama says. But I do not want to marry him, Richard. He is old, and so stiff, and I swear he makes me feel, well, quite stupid when I have to talk to him."

She paused for a moment and frowned. "Why are you both laughing?"

"Only at the absurdity of your mother, my love," said Richard. "My Lord Gloucester may well be contemplating marriage, but it is with quite a different bride in mind."

"Oh!" said Charlotte, and Abigail smiled at the note of disappointment in the younger woman's voice. "Perhaps you did not know that he danced twice with me tonight. Or that he stayed to talk with me without a chaperone for over half an hour."

"You didn't need a chaperone when you were in full view of the room, darling. Depend upon it, the Earl has no thought of proposing to you."

Despite her assurances that she had no wish to marry anyone but her true love, Charlotte appeared to be quite deflated by this. "Well, if you think so, Richard," she said without conviction.

Abigail, very much looking forward to relaying this anecdote to Lord Gloucester, rallied to Charlotte's cause. "Well I for one think that the Earl has behaved quite scandalously towards you. It is no wonder that his attentions could be misconstrued. But as much as I am sure he holds you in deep regard – after all you are a perfectly respectable choice for him! – the Earl is not the type of man to accept an unwilling bride. If he knew that you were in love with another, he would not dream of coming between you."

Charlotte brightened a touch at this speech. "No, I don't think he is the type, is he? He would not come between Richard and me." Her shoulders sagged. "But Mama will not like it. She is convinced I should be a Countess, or if not, then I should marry a Duke instead."

Richard nodded confirmation of this point to Abigail. "It was Lady Harden that set it about that I was a penniless rake. My friends have done their best to refute the rumours, but mud, as they say, tends to stick. Were it not for the Putneys and the Loughcrofts, she may well have seen me ostracised from the Ton."

"Odious woman," muttered Abigail, then apologised to Charlotte for insulting her mother.

"I perfectly understand, Mrs Merriweather. Mama – Mama is not well liked, even by our own family. I have not seen Grandmother since my presentation, when Mama and her quarrelled about my outfit." She looked down at her dress and gave an unhappy sigh. "I wish Grandmother had won that battle. She refused to forward another penny to Mama and said she washed her hands of the whole matter. I wish I could live with her in Bath, only then I would not see Richard."

"No use worrying over that now," said Captain Rowlands, capturing her hand in his. "The problem is what to do about us. Your mother made it quite clear that she was offended by my offering to marry you, and short of my being elevated to the peerage, I can think of nothing that I can do to make my suit acceptable."

"No, and I don't think it is very kind of us to wish both your uncles and all of your cousins dead, is it, even if it did mean you would become a Baronet."

Abigail regarded the couple in thoughtful silence for a while.

"It would be a perfectly respectable match," she eventually murmured, more to herself than to the couple before her. "Richard's birth is genteel, and his fortune acceptable. If someone would stand their friend, maybe sponsor them back into society, the thing could be done."

The soldier looked up at her. "What are you thinking, Abby?"

"That there's only one thing you can do. Elope."

There was a stunned silence, followed quickly by both lovers chattering at once.

"Good God, Abby, what sort of ramshackle libertine do you think I am?"

"Oh but I could not! Mama would never let me out of her sight long enough!"

Abigail raised her hands to shush them both. "Will you listen to me for one moment, my dears? I don't mean that you should fly to the border; indeed I suspect it is not at all comfortable and quite unnecessary."

"Well if you don't mean a flight to the border, what do you mean?"

Abigail nodded towards Charlotte. "She's twenty-

one. You don't need her mother's consent to marry.
All you need is a special licence."

Charlotte blinked a few times. "Could it be that
easy?"

It was Richard who shook his head. "No,
Charlotte. If we were to get married in such a way
then you would be cut off from the Ton. As much
as I want you to be my wife, I could not do that to
you."

"But I would not mind if it meant that we could
be together. I am sure that I would like following the
Drum, or even living in Yorkshire if I had to."

Richard, much moved by this tribute, enveloped
his love in his arms and kissed her forehead. "You
are a darling, Charlotte, but I could not take you away
from your friends and family like that."

"You wouldn't have to," announced Abigail,
playing her trump card. "Honestly, Richard, credit
me with some intelligence. All you need is Seraphinia
Harden."

Another silence.

"Grandmother?" asked Charlotte, her brow
creased up in a frown.

Abigail nodded. "Emma told me that her Aunt
would do anything to get back at your mother,
they've been at each other's throats for years. If

Emma wrote a letter explaining everything, and the two of you ran away to Bath, then I am sure that your Grandmother would take pity on you, and happily consent to your wedding. Your mother would not be able to do anything about it, either, for if your Grandmother came back to London with you, why, she has far more influence over the Ton that your mother has ever had."

Richard nodded slowly. "And she would be able to confirm that I am not the penniless rake that Lady Harden claims me to be. No one would think it odd if Seraphinia came to London to show her support for us. Lady Harden may lose face out of this, but no one could blame Charlotte if her grandmother leant us her aid."

Charlotte transferred her gaze between them, hope in her eyes. "We could do it, then? We could get married? Oh Richard, I would like that more than anything in the world!"

"Then it is settled," said Abigail. "I will speak to Emma and convince her to write to her aunt, explaining everything. We can be ready within a week or two."

Charlotte visibly paled. "Weeks? Oh no, please Mrs Merriweather, we cannot possibly leave it for weeks. Mama will have told everyone that the Earl is to offer for me. I shall die of mortification if he does not ask me to be his wife, and if he does, well, what am I to do then?"

Richard added his concerns. "Lady Harden has made it clear that I am not welcome near her daughter. The longer we leave it the harder it will be to arrange; she disapproves of your friendship with Charlotte just as much as she does of mine, and if Emma goes into confinement early, then we will be undone."

"Mama thinks you too dashing, Mrs Merriweather," said Charlotte, "but I do not agree. I think you quite the kindest, bravest woman I have ever met. I have never been so in awe of anyone as I was when you rode in that balloon across London, and weren't the least bit afraid to be alone with those two men for hours!"

"It was hardly hours," said Abigail, feeling her cheeks flame, "and the whole incident is best forgotten."

"Forgotten!" squeaked Charlotte, and she reached out to grab Abigail's hands. "I wish I were brave enough to be an Aeronaut! You are just like Mrs Sage, only more genteel!"

"Hush, my darling, you are embarrassing Mrs Merriweather," said Captain Rowlands, although the effect was ruined by the laughter in his voice.

"The balloon ascension is quite irrelevant in this matter," said Abigail with as much dignity as she could muster. "We were talking about your future happiness. If you are both set on this course, and determined that you must go as soon as possible, then I suggest we do not delay at all, and set out tomorrow."

"But... but is it possible? How would I get my things together? Mama would find out!"

Abigail softened, and squeezed Charlotte's hand. "I promise you, my dear, that there is nothing to worry about at all. Tomorrow I will find a way to get you out of your house without your mother or a maid to guard you, just see if I don't! Now, dry your tears and go back out to the ball; it would not do for your Mama to miss you."

Richard stepped over and kissed Charlotte lightly on the cheek. "Do as Mrs Merriweather says, darling. It will be all right and tight, I promise."

"If... if you say so," murmured Charlotte. She straightened her dress and went to the door. She paused, and looked back at them both. "I know you must think I am a poor-spirited creature, but if you can get me away from Mama then I promise I will do anything to be with Richard, even if we have to fly in a balloon to get away from her. Now, that would show her that I know what I am about!"

And on this note, she left.

"Richard Rowlands you owe me a debt of undying gratitude for getting me involved in this," said Abigail, folding her arms across her chest.

The soldier flashed her a rueful grin. "I know, fairest Juno, I know!"

"Charlotte Harden? Really?"

His smile faded, his expression defensive. "I know what you are thinking, Abby, but not every man wants to marry a firecracker. Charlotte may not be up to the snuff, but she is a darling, and I love her to distraction."

"You don't have to explain the absurdity of falling in love to me, old friend," said Abigail with a sigh, "I meant no disrespect to Charlotte. She is indeed a lovely girl – although promise me that you will get her into some fashionable clothes and never, ever let her wear pink again!"

"Done," smiled the soldier. "Do you think this plan of yours will work?"

"So long as I can convince Emma to take part, then yes." She thought about that for a moment. "I suppose I could ask Gloucester."

Richard shook his head. "Oh no you don't, Abigail. If you breathe a word of this to him I shall never forgive you. The man dislikes me almost as much as the Old Bat does."

"If he has a poor opinion of you then I am sure it is your own fault for acting up to the part of a libertine," snapped Abigail, annoyed at his abuse of the Earl's character. "He simply does not know the truth of the matter, and if he did I am sure he would lend you his unqualified support."

"I know you have a soft spot for him, my dear, but trust me on this: he would far prefer to prevent this marriage than to condone it."

Abigail started to argue, but stopped herself as the truth of these words hit home. "Yes, you're probably right. It would take too long to explain it to him in such a way that he would offer his support. Very well, I won't say a word to him about where we are going."

"We?"

"If we are aiming to keep this elopement as above board as possible then I can hardly let you ride off unchaperoned, can I? I will accompany you both to Bath, and once Charlotte is comfortably established with her Grandmother I will return home by post."

Richard stared at her for a long time. "You are a wonderful friend, Abby. I just hope that this affair does not damage you. I had no right to ask for your assistance."

"Fudge! What else are friends for if not to drag you into their scrapes and help you out of your own?"

He laughed, then impulsively grabbed her up in his arms and swung her about him. "Dearest, darling Abby! I'm going to be married!" He laughed again, and planted a kiss onto her cheek just as the door was opened, flooding the small room with candlelight.

"Well of all the vulgar, indecent behaviour I have ever witnessed!" the foghorn voice of Lady Harden announced.

Richard and Abigail pulled apart, staring in horror as Lady Harden stood, hands planted firmly on her hips, in the open doorway. Behind her were several other guests, already whispering and sniggering.

"I would expect nothing better of you, Mrs Merriweather, but to think that I allowed you, Captain Rowlands, to befriend my daughter is quite beyond the pale!"

Richard failed to keep the anger and contempt from his face. "Perhaps you would like to be the first to congratulate me on my forthcoming marriage, Lady Harden."

Lady Harden gave a contemptuous snort. "Then that little harridan has done better for herself than I expected. Good riddance to the both of you."

"I thank you for your kind words and blessing," snapped Abigail, barely able to keep her rage under control. More and more people were gathering just outside of the room, desperate to find out what was going on.

"That will do, Eliza!" Lady Putney came to the

doorway, unceremoniously pushing Lady Harden out of her way. She reached out her hands to the Captain and Abigail. "You have quite ruined the romantic moment that the dear, dear Captain here begged me to set up for him. I hope that she had time to accept your proposal, Captain Rowlands, and that you will forgive Lady Harden for misunderstanding the situation."

"Thank you, my Lady," said Richard, accepting her involvement without as much as a blink. "My love has agreed to do me the honour of becoming my wife and we hope to be married immediately."

"Oh do you?" snapped Lady Harden. "I suppose you are happy to settle for what you can get. Does she know that only this morning you called at my lodging to ask if-"

"I said that will do," announced Lady Putney with a growl that any drill sergeant could be proud of. "You are forgetting yourself, Eliza. If you cannot bring yourself to wish the couple happy then you should say nothing at all."

"Which couple happy?" asked Emma. "I can hear you halfway down the ballroom, Lady Harden. Who is to be married?"

"Mrs Merriweather and Captain Rowlands," said Lady Putney. "The Captain enlisted my help for a surprise betrothal, but Lady Harden interrupted them and got quite the wrong end of the stick."

"Betrothal?" whispered Emma. She glanced up into the face of her brother, who had escorted her down to the commotion.

"Please accept my felicitations on your impending nuptials," said Gloucester, his voice unusually quiet. He did not meet Abby's gaze.

"George," she said before she could stop herself, reaching out to him. He flinched, then turned and walked away.

Captain Rowlands took hold of her hand. "Abby, I-" but she shook her head and he stopped speaking.

Emma stared at them both for a long minute, her eyes narrowed. "Abigail darling, I am so sorry to interrupt but I am afraid I'm not feeling at all the thing. If Captain Rowlands would like to come to the house for luncheon tomorrow, then we can celebrate properly. Lend me your arm, dearest. Lady Putney, I am sure you will forgive us for leaving early?"

Lady Putney was all consideration. With a weak smile at Captain Rowlands, Abby allowed herself to be led away by the Loughcrofts. Her eyes scanned the crowds as they walked to the front door, but Gloucester appeared to have gone.

CHAPTER EIGHT

"You're helping them do *what?*" screeched Emma. Abigail winced, rubbing at her ear pointedly.

"I'm helping them reach your Aunt Seraphinia so that they can be married. It is a perfectly respectable match, they are very much in love and what's more, Charlotte is unlikely to do any better for herself than Richard."

"But Lady Putney said that you were marrying Captain Rowlands."

"Lady Putney, bless her, was trying to help out after that Old Bat Harden dared to accuse me of being a lightskirt." Abigail sighed. "It was well-intentioned of her, but look at the mess that has come of it."

Emma shook her head. "Poor George, he must be heartbroken. You must tell him the truth immediately."

"I can't, dearest. I promised that I would not breathe a word of this to your brother. He already thinks Richard is ramshackle, Lord knows how he'd react to this. I don't think he would betray the couple, but you know very well he might try to stop them."

Alistair, leaning back against the seat on the other side of the coach, joined in the conversation. "Daresay he would. Grand fellow, but a bit of a stickler."

"Yes, and what's more, neither of you can tell him, either, because I'm begging you not to!"

"But he thinks that it is you who's getting married to Captain Rowlands! Oh Abby, the timing!"

Abigail thought back to Gloucester asking to have a private word with her on the morrow, and felt her heart breaking.

"Well, no use crying over these things," she said in a vain attempt to sound cheerful. "I daresay he'd have grown tired of my pranks within a week, and will shortly congratulate himself on his lucky escape."

"If you could just explain it to him," sighed Emma.

"I can't, dearest, at least not until after the thing is done."

"It might well be too late by then," sighed Emma in a morose tone. It felt like a knife in Abby's gut, but she said nothing.

"Never mind my affairs, let's talk about Richard and Charlotte. Will you help them, Emma? It is such a little thing that you would have to do."

"You call writing a letter to Aunt Seraphinia, demanding she aid a pair of runaways in a clandestine marriage 'a small thing'? Not to mention kidnapping Charlotte out from under her mother's nose? No, no trouble at all!"

"Well I never thought you would be so mean spirited!" said Abigail, crossing her arms.

"Not mean spirited," interrupted Alistair as Emma let out a squeak of outrage, "just that she's as bad as her brother at times."

Abigail frowned. "Drat, I never thought of that."

"Excuse me, but I am sitting right here," sniffed Emma, "and I am sure that I know not what you mean."

Alistair patted her knee with a fond smile. "I love you dearly, but you're not the sort to do anything that's not by the book. Abigail was quite wrong to ask you to help and put you in a moral quandary. Not the thing at all! But don't worry yourself about it, my darling; I'm sure that between us Abby and I can work everything out!"

"You are going to help Charlotte Harden elope?" asked Emma, incredulity soaking her words.

"Why wouldn't I? Never could stand the Old Bat, and if the girl's out the way then Lady Harden won't come sniffing around you and George all the time, trying to get him to propose. Better for us all."

"Dearest Alistair, your altruism never fails to astound me," laughed Abigail.

Emma looked angry. "I think you are both very unfair. Just because I don't think people should do something that's bad ton doesn't mean I lack pluck."

"Never suggested it!" said Alistair. "Just meant Abby was wrong to put you in a position like this."

"No she was not. Abby is my friend, and what's more, Charlotte is related to me. There is nothing more natural than my desire to help ensure her future happiness. I shall write that letter to my Aunt Seraphinia and, what's more, I shall go to the Harden's tomorrow and invite Charlotte to come driving with me. I am only sorry that my pregnancy means that I cannot drive with the couple to Bath myself. So there!" She sat back into her seat and glared at them both, as if willing them to try and challenge her.

"If that's what you want, my dearest wife, then naturally I shall support you in your decision," said Alistair with a straight face. He threw a wink at Abby, who just about managed to smother a laugh with her hand.

*

The following morning found the Loughcroft household up and about at an unreasonably early hour. Abigail threw herself into the plan to help her friends, and tried very hard not to think about Lord

Gloucester, or the pain she had seen in his face.

An urgent missive was sent to Captain Rowlands, ordering him to have a chaise and four ready and waiting at the appointed hour. She paused, briefly wondering how he would be able to excuse himself from military duties, but this was an area outside her expertise and she decided that he would know his own business best in that area.

Once this letter was in the care of a footman she hurriedly packed her case with essentials for an overnight trip to Bath and asked Martha to lay out her favourite carriage dress. Between Emma and herself they managed to put together a second bag of clothing for Charlotte, trusting that her grandmother would see fit to take her to a dressmaker at her earliest convenience.

Emma had decided that she would have more luck in wresting Charlotte from Lady Harden if she visited her cousin alone, pointing out that since Lady Harden had quite loudly called Abigail a harridan, she was unlikely to allow her into the house, let alone leave Charlotte alone with her. Alistair escorted his wife on her visit, leaving Abigail to kick her heels at home.

The flowers from George were everywhere and their scent followed her about the house, taunting her at every turn. She tried several times to compose him a letter, attempting to explain what had happened without breaking her word to Richard, but every time they ended up screwed into little balls and tossed to the floor. Eventually, she managed to write,

My Dearest George,

I know how things must appear to you, and that my behaviour once again seems quite scandalous. I am obliged to go out of town for a day or two, but I promise to explain all to you on my return.

Yours, Abigail

The Loughcrofts returned home just as she handed this letter to the footman with a request to deliver it as soon as she left the house. Charlotte Harden practically flew into the hallway, grasping hold of Abigail's hands so tightly they turned white under the pressure.

"Mrs Merriweather you are quite wonderful! Indeed, so is Lady Loughcroft, for how she managed to cajole Mama into letting me go with her, I will never understand!"

"That was easy, my dear," said Emma as she came into the hallway. "I simply explained that I wanted us to get to know each other better, and that I should like to be upon the most sisterly of terms with you."

"That's what I mean," said Charlotte. "You already know me quite well, so I have no notion why you should suddenly want to know me better now."

"Lady Loughcroft allowed your mother to believe

that she was willing to encourage your engagement to her brother," explained Abigail in a kind voice. She almost laughed at the look of alarm that appeared on Miss Harden's face. "No no, she is helping you to marry Captain Rowlands, but if your mother thinks that she wants you to marry Lord Gloucester, then she will not object to letting you out of her sight."

Charlotte blinked a few times before realisation dawned. She turned to Emma and shook her hand. "You are so clever, Lady Loughcroft! I would never have thought of that."

"Well, be that as it may, we should get going. Is everything arranged, Abby?"

Abigail nodded. "Just let me collect my bag and we can go."

Alistair drove the three ladies through Hyde Park to the rendezvous point, where Captain Rowlands was waiting for them. He wore a plain suit and a greatcoat with several capes thrown across his shoulders, and Abigail could not help but notice that he did not look quite so impressive out of his regimentals. Charlotte, however, did not appear to share this view, and it was with obvious effort that she refrained from flinging herself into his arms.

"We will give you two hours," said Emma. "After that, we will tell Lady Harden that Charlotte desired to visit the library, but when we returned for her she had gone, and left only her letter. Have you explained everything in the note, my dear?"

Charlotte swallowed, but nodded. "Yes, and I hope that she will not be too mad at you, after all you have done for us!"

"Nothing of the sort," said Alistair cheerfully. "I'll tell her my wife left you in my charge. Your Mama won't dare argue with me."

"Would she really not?" asked Charlotte, seeming very impressed by anyone who could face her mother without concern. "You are one of the bravest men I have ever met, my Lord."

Captain Rowlands helped the two ladies settle themselves into the chaise. He shook hands with both Lord and Lady Loughcroft, thanking them for their help. "You did not need to lend us your aid, but I am thankful for it."

"Abby didn't leave us a choice," said Alistair, and the two men shared a grin.

"Now don't forget my letter, Captain," reminded Emma. "Aunt Seraphinia is a dragon when she wants to be, but I've tried to explain it to her and ten to one she'll support you if only to upset her daughter-in-law."

"I depend upon your powers of diplomacy, my Lady, and thank you once again."

He climbed up into the carriage, all three occupants waving goodbye as they set out on their journey to Bath.

Emma cuddled into her husband as they watched the chaise and four disappear into the distance. "Do you think we should go to George now?"

Alistair shook his head. "No, not with the speed of his greys. Give it an hour, then we'll go call on him."

"Do you think it will work? Telling him that Captain Rowlands has forced Abigail to run away with him, I mean?"

"If it doesn't then he's not worthy of her, regardless of whether he's your brother or not."

Emma nodded. "You're right, of course. Though it is terribly vulgar of us to interfere like this."

"Us?" asked Alistair with a wry smile. "My darling wife, if Gloucester ever calls me out over this escapade, I'm going to say it was all your idea."

CHAPTER NINE

The drive out to Bath began well. Although Abigail's heart was in turmoil she was clever enough not to let it show, and the happy couple beside her were in high spirits.

It took less than an hour for things to go wrong.

Charlotte, it turned out, was a poor traveller. The further they drove the quieter she became until eventually her face took on a sickly green colour. Richard would have slowed the carriage at that point, perhaps even stop for refreshments, but the girl would have none of it. She was still sure that her mother would somehow uncover their flight, and had visions of the Bow Street Runners chasing after them and arresting Richard for kidnap.

Two hours into the drive, Richard decided enough was enough and determined to pull into the nearest inn. Charlotte made a weak protest, but as neither Abigail nor the Captain had any wish for her to be sick in the chaise, she was overruled.

While Richard went with the ostlers to make sure the horses were properly cared for, Abigail helped the sickly Charlotte into the private parlour. The Innkeeper's wife soon appeared with refreshments, but one look at Charlotte had her shaking her head and tutting.

"Poor thing needs to lay down. I can have guest chamber ready in a moment, Ma'am, if you think you can spare the time."

"Yes, that is a very good idea. Thank you," said Abigail.

Charlotte began to protest. "But we have so far to go!"

"Nonsense," said Abigail, putting Miss Harden firmly into the care of the Innkeeper's wife. "A quiet lie down for an hour, and you will be right as rain. We have plenty of time."

"Well if you think so," said Charlotte, her voice weak. "Oh I am sorry for being poor-spirited."

Abigail smiled at her and squeezed her hand. "You are not in the least poor-spirited. It has been a hard few days for you, and the carriage is badly sprung. It is a wonder that I do not feel as ill as you!"

"Perhaps," said Charlotte as she was led from the room. She looked over her shoulder and added in an awestruck voice, "but I suppose nothing could shake you after riding in a balloon."

Ten minutes later Richard came into the parlour, surprised that Charlotte was not there. He frowned when Abigail told him she was lying down, but agreed it was the best thing to do. "I had no notion she was such a poor traveller. Still, an hour's rest should not set us back too badly, we've made good time so far."

Abigail agreed, and begged him to sit down.

They both enjoyed the coffee and cake provided by the Innkeeper and complimented his wife on her excellent baking skills. That worthy gentlemen thanked them, and left them to share their refreshments in peace.

"I... I have not had the chance to apologise to you for last night," said Richard as soon as they were alone. "I would not have blamed you for crying off from this whole escapade."

"What, and shy away from the chance of making yet another scandal? Never!" said Abigail lightly. Richard was not buying it.

"You can't bam me, my dear, I've known you this last ten years or more."

"Oh, how rude of you to betray my real age! And there was I, believing you to be an officer and a gentleman. For shame!"

"Dash it, Abigail, will you be serious for a moment? I would not have ruined your own chances for all the world. When Charlotte and I are safely married, I will return to London and call on the Earl. I will explain to him, I will make him see what happened."

"That is kind of you, Richard, but if Gloucester believes I am the type of woman to play fast and loose with him like this, then perhaps he is not worthy of me after all."

"Don't you love him, Abby?"

She smiled, but it felt brittle. "Feelings are of no consequence. Besides, if Lady Loughcroft finds she does not need me once the baby is born, then I may well return to Yorkshire sooner than planned."

Richard looked like he wanted to continue the conversation, but Abigail was glad he held his peace. It was easy enough to turn his thoughts back to his betrothed, and with very little effort was able to draw him out on his plans for the future.

It was part way through these musings that a commotion came from outside the Inn, and the sound of raised voices echoed into their private parlour.

"What the devil could this mean?" muttered Richard, and stood up. Before he could take three paces, the door to the private parlour flew open and the Earl of Gloucester strode into the room.

"My Lord, what are you-" began the Captain, but never got the chance to finish. The Earl swung for him, planting a flush hit that sent the Soldier sprawling out onto the floor.

"George, what are you doing?" shouted Abigail in

horror.

The Earl, however, was not listening. He strode over to Abigail, grabbing hold of her shoulders. "Don't do this, Abby! Whatever this scoundrel has told you, don't believe a word of it! If you must marry someone then for God's sake, marry me!"

Abigail, paralysed with shock, was unable to speak. She stared into his angry face, for the first time in her life completely at a loss for what to say. George misunderstood her silence, the look of anger turning to anguish. "Damn it, Abby, don't you know that I love you?"

Richard, who had by this stage climbed back to his feet and placed several feet between himself and the Earl, nursed his jaw. "I believe that my debt to you is repaid in full, fairest Juno."

George, recalled to the soldier's presence, turned to face him with murder in his eyes. "You misbegotten cur," he growled, "I should beat you."

"No George, please, you've got it all wrong," said Abigail as she grabbed hold of his arm. Much struck by the humour of the situation, she let out a little giggle that had the effect of stopping the Earl dead in his tracks. He turned to look at her, obviously confused, but before she had a chance to explain anything to him the door flew open for a second time, and Charlotte Harden ran into the room like a classical fury.

"How dare you come after us! You have no right at all, and I don't care what Mama says, nothing could induce me to turn from this course of action, so you have quite wasted your time! If you touch a single hair on Richard's head, then I swear that I shall... I shall *shoot* you!"

Abigail couldn't help herself and started laughing. She bit down on her own knuckles in an attempt to hide it, but with little success. Lord Gloucester appeared rooted to the spot, his mouth opening and closing like a fish, while Charlotte stood in front of Captain Rowlands looking every inch an Amazonian Princess, which was impressive considering she was dressed in a poorly fitted carriage dress of drab, and barely reached the captain's shoulder in her bare feet.

"I have to tell you my dearest darling Charlotte, that I have never loved you quite so much as I do this moment," said Richard, beaming with pride. His fiancé turned adoring eyes up at him, professing her own love.

"What the devil are you doing here?" asked George, still staring at Miss Harden as though not quite believing his eyes.

Charlotte's wrath was quick to resurface. She glared at the Earl with such hatred that Abigail was quite glad the girl did not, in fact, have a pistol with which to shoot him.

"You may well ask that, my Lord," she said,

making 'Lord' sound like a curse, "for I am sure it never crossed your mind that I would prefer to be a plain Mrs than a Countess, did it? Well it is the truth, and nothing can induce me to marry you, for I love Richard, and if you tied me up in a tower for the rest of my days I still wouldn't marry you, so… so there!"

It appeared to take George a moment or two to process this tangled speech, for there was a short pause before he began to reply. "Marry you? Good God, Charlotte, I never had any intention of- ouch!"

The exclamation of pain was caused by Abigail, who made contact with the back of his calf muscle with a well-aimed kick. She thanked the Heavens he was an intelligent man, for she was able to convey everything she wanted him to know with little more than a meaningful glance at the other couple.

George, his entire demeanour shifting, extended his hand to Charlotte. "What I meant to say was that I never had any intention of coming between two people who love each other so much. Indeed, I was misled about this entire situation – I had no notion at all that Captain Rowlands and you had formed an attachment. I promise faithfully that I will not force you to marry me, Miss Harden. Indeed, I would never forgive myself if such a thing were to happen!"

Charlotte lifted her chin and looked mulish. "Are you saying that you would not want to marry me, sir?"

"Not in the slightest, I can assure you!" he replied. Abigail dug her elbow into his spine. "What I mean to say is that I would never take an unwilling bride!"

"That... that is very good of you," said Charlotte. She took hold of Richard's hand in hers, interlacing their fingers. "So you won't stop us going to Bath, then?"

"No, of course not, though I'll be dashed if I know why you are going there at all."

"Your Aunt Seraphinia," supplied Abigail. George looked more lost than ever.

"The only person who frightens Mama is my Grandmother," explained Charlotte. "And perhaps Lord Loughcroft, but then he cannot sponsor me so it does not signify. Your sister has written a letter to my Grandmother explaining everything, so I can be married under her approval, and no one will be able to say anything about it because she's one of the most important ladies in the Ton."

"Emma wrote a letter..." repeated Gloucester. His brow darkened. "Well of all the underhand, devious minxes I have ever met! Aye, and Alistair, too! I'll wring both their necks when I get back to London."

Abigail gasped. "Emma told you where to find us?"

Richard was the only person in the room who seemed to find this amusing. "I suspect that Lady

Loughcroft told you a lot more than just our direction, my Lord?"

"Well of all the poor turns to serve a friend!" exclaimed Abigail, folding her arms across her chest. "It would serve her right if I didn't return in time for the birth after all!"

Charlotte looked blankly at each of them. "What is wrong? Has Lady Loughcroft betrayed us? But why would she do such a thing after helping me escape from Mama?"

George shook his head. "No need to worry, Miss Harden, rather my sister has played a very poor joke on me. Now, I collect that you and Captain Rowlands here are in a hurry to get to Bath. I suggest that you do not hesitate to get back onto the road. After all, if I found you so quickly, there is no saying who else may be following you!"

Captain Rowlands began to protest, but Charlotte was frightened enough by this prospect to start babbling on about Bow Street Runners, and demanding that Richard drive her to Bath that instant.

"I am afraid that you will have to go the rest of the way without Mrs Merriweather," announced Lord Gloucester, "I will need her support when I face Lady Harden, and explain that I am not to marry Charlotte."

The soldier laughed as the Earl herded the couple

towards the door. "Doing rather too brown there, my Lord!"

"Richard shush, let us be on our way!" demanded Charlotte, paying no heed to the conversation. "Thank you for everything, Mrs Merriweather; if anyone can stand up to Mama, it is you!"

"May I wish you happy, Lord Gloucester?" asked Richard as he crossed through the doorway and out into the hall.

"I dashed well hope so. Now be gone, and give my love to Aunt Seraphinia!" and with that, he slammed the door shut.

Alone in the private parlour with him, Abigail suddenly felt very shy and very nervous. She smoothed down her skirts, trying to dispel an imaginary crease with her hands.

"Abigail," whispered George as he approached her. She took a step backwards.

"Please, my Lord, you need not. I have been very foolish, and allowed myself to get quite carried away with things."

"Yes, I would agree with that. It seems to be a rather a fundamental part of your character."

She winced. "Well, never let it be said that I am dull!"

"I would agree with that, too. You are quite the most irritating, scandalous, bewitching, adorable female I have ever met, and I'll be dashed if I can live another moment without you."

Abigail let out a little sob, and he caught her up in his arms.

"I am so sorry I could not tell you where I had gone," she told him, "but I gave Richard my word that I would help him, and then what was I to do-"

"Save to come up with the most outrageous plan of yours to date!" he finished for her, but it was said with a smile.

"So you do understand," she sighed, feeling like the weight of the world had been lifted from her shoulders.

"What I understand, my darling, is that men do the silliest things for love, like chase half way down the Bath road after the woman they want to marry, only to discover that she hasn't run off at all."

Abigail gave a choke of laughter. "Oh, that was infamous of Emma and Alistair! Why on earth would I elope with Captain Rowlands if I was already engaged to him? It makes no sense!"

"To be honest, my darling, I wasn't thinking very straight when they told me." He tucked a hand under her chin and gently tilted her head upwards until she was facing him. "My beautiful Abby, I have been such a fool. Will you marry me?"

A fat teardrop escaped from her eye and ran down her cheek. "Yes, oh yes George, I would like that more than anything!"

With a shocking disregard for the state of her dress and hair, George crushed her against him as he kissed her with a passion she had not known he possessed. When he reluctantly released her she attempted to straighten her outfit with limited success.

"Look at the state of me! George, you cannot drive me back to London looking like this; what on earth would people say?"

"Who on earth said I was taking you back to London?" he asked, a wicked gleam in his eye.

It was Abigail's turn to be confused. "But where else would we go?"

"For my part, I plan to take you to the nearest church and get the parson to marry us here and now. Dash it, Abby, I nearly lost you once, I'm not letting you out my sight again until you are my legally wedded wife."

"But...but the licence..."

"I have a special licence right here in my pocket, my darling." He laughed when he saw the look on her face, and then leant in to kiss her once again.

"Are you shocked, Abigail? Do you think you are the only one with a propensity to be dashing?"

"Dashing!" exclaimed Abigail, halfway between joy and horror, "George, you are positively *scandalous*!"

NOTES FROM THE AUTHOR

Thank you for reading The Dashing Widow – I hope that you enjoyed it! I cannot express enough how much it means to me that not only did you buy this book, that you then read it, and now you are reading these waffling, over-excited notes from me!

I have always been a reader, and have no preference when it comes to genre, time period, or even style so long as the story is one that will hook me in. Even as a child, my mum would complain that grounding me was fairly useless as I saw the opportunity to snuggle up with a book as a treat as opposed to a punishment. I still feel like that, to be honest. Books will always be these magical gateways that take me to other times, worlds and places that I treasure.

This book, strictly speaking, didn't come about because of my own love of books, however. It came about because of my mum. She's a lifelong Georgette Heyer fan (she's a woman of good taste), but she's gone through multiple copies of every book, since she reads them until they quite literally fall to pieces. We can quote lines at each other, and she's the only person I know who understands what I mean when I announce after several bottles of wine, "I may be three sheets to the wind, my love, but I've not yet shot the cat."

A few years ago, I came up with the idea of writing a short regency romance, in the style of Georgette Heyer, for my mum to enjoy as a birthday gift. She's a tough critic, but she loved it enough to badger me into publishing it. I never thought anyone else would be interested in it, let alone read it all the way through, and yet here you are reading my author notes – and I just cannot express how much that means to me.

I have to admit, though, that when it comes to the Regency period I am only an enthusiastic amateur – and therefore I occasionally make mistakes. Please, if you find something that I have messed up in the books, such as using the wrong title, or naming a street that wasn't built until the 1900s, please reach out to me at Elizabeth@ElizabethBramwell.com so that I can correct any errors. The beauty of indie publishing is that I have the freedom to update at any time, and of course I absolutely adore learning more about this period. I thank every reader who has reached out to me from the bottom of my heart, and it's nice to have made a few friends along the way.

You can also check out my website at www.ElizabethBramwell.com where there is an up to date list of my books, information about the Regency Period, and a link to join my Reader Group.

In the meantime, please read on to see the first chapter of my next book, *The Foolish Friend*, out now!

THE FOOLISH FRIEND

CHAPTER ONE

James Douglas, 4th Baron of Cottingham, smiled from the doorway of his lifelong friend's front parlour. He'd been able to convince the Marquess of Shropshire's butler, who had known him since he'd still worn leading-strings, that it would be a great joke for him to enter the room unannounced, and be able to surprise both Lady Shropshire and her granddaughter, Lady Henrietta.

So far, it seemed like it had been a good plan. It was early in the Season, but already the Shropshire's afternoon callers numbered in the low teens. Lady Henrietta (although he struggled to think of her as anything but a feisty eight-year-old demanding to be called Henry) sat with a few other young ladies beside the window, their heads together as they giggled over something secretive.

Her grandmother, the redoubtable Marchioness of Shropshire, held court towards the centre of the room, where half a dozen matrons of the Ton and a smattering of bored-looking young men drank tea and made polite small talk. No doubt the poor gentlemen would be happier talking to some of the attractive misses sat at the window, but manners demanded they visit with Lady Shropshire rather than her granddaughter's friends.

He walked into the room quietly and without fuss, intending to take a chair beside the Marchioness and see how long it would take for her to notice his presence, when Henry chose that moment to glance in his direction, and then managed to quite ruin his little trick.

"James!" she cried out, jumping to her feet. "I didn't hear you announced!"

He gave her a rueful smile as everyone turned to look at him. "You haven't changed a bit in the last year, Henry, and still manage to ruin a good joke when you have the opportunity."

A couple of the gentlemen laughed, and Henry blushed deeply. As she sank down to her seat he wondered if he'd hurt her feelings, but before he could reassure her that he'd only been teasing, his attention was claimed by the Marchioness.

"Cottingham, my dear boy, when did you return?" she said, extending her thin hand towards him as he approached. "Your mother must be so happy to have you back in the fold."

"I think she's just relieved that I came back in one piece," he said as he bowed over the older Lady's hand. "As much as I loved Montreal, I confess that it is good to be home."

"We are glad to have your company once again, my boy. It was quite selfish of you to leave us for an entire year; even Henrietta pined for your escort around Hyde Park, didn't you, my love?"

Henry, whose cheeks were still flushed, gave a weak smile in his direction. "Who doesn't like to spend time with their friends?"

Several of the young women were studying him with open curiosity, and he wondered if he had danced with any of them before his departure. He smiled and nodded in their direction, just in case.

"You are all acquainted with Lord Cottingham, I believe?" said Lady Shropshire, gesturing at the entire room with one hand. "He's been in Canada or some such place for the last year, but I've known the boy since he was still in the cradle. His lands march alongside those of Shropshire House, of course, and we've missed him like he was one of the family."

There were a few murmured welcomes, and many bows exchanged, but Lady Shropshire's guests took her hint and began to leave. Henry kissed the last of her friends on the cheek, and only the three of them remained.

"You didn't have to cut short your gathering on my account," said James as he settled himself into a chair.

"Nonsense, I was bored practically to tears by their inane conversation," said Lady Shropshire. "It's too early in the Season for any real gossip to have begun, so most of them are more interested in learning what they can about my great-nephew, Gloucester."

James glanced at Henry for an explanation, but she raised her brows in surprise.

"I told you in my letters, James. Cousin Gloucester ran off and married a trade widow called Abby near the end of last Season in a havey-cavey manner."

"Ah, I remember now," he said, but Henry narrowed her gaze at him.

"You never read that letter, did you?"

He felt his cheeks warm a little, and resisted the urge to tug at his cravat. "I'm sorry, Henry; I was dashed busy while in Montreal learning all about the estate's investments in the Hudson Bay Company, not to mention getting my brother settled into his new role out there. I'm afraid that I didn't have the leisure to read."

"And on the ship back?" she asked, something between anger and hurt dancing in her eyes. "I suppose in all those endless hours in your cabin you were too busy as well."

"Hush my dear," admonished her grandmother. "Gentlemen have a quite surprising amount of work they need to accomplish in any given day, and no doubt he would have read your letters if he'd had the time. Isn't that so, Cottingham?"

The sharp look resting on Lady Shropshire's face suggested that she didn't mean a word of what she'd said, causing his cheeks to heat further. "Yes, of course, although I'm dashed sorry for it, Henry. I'll read them as soon as I'm home, how's that?"

The smile Henry flashed was a sickly one, and James had the uncomfortable feeling that he'd hurt her feelings once again.

"No need for that now, as I'm sure you'll be twice as busy in London as you were in Montreal. Besides, you're here now, so I suppose I can just tell you everything you need to know about what you missed, including my cousin's marriage."

"I would like that," he said, and was relieved to see Lady Shropshire give a small nod of approval.

"Not that there was any reason for Gloucester to run off the way he did," sniffed the Marchioness. "He's made it harder for his new wife to be accepted by the Ton, of course, but the family is determined to support the new Countess of Gloucester, and anyone who chooses not to accept her shall incur my censure!"

"And that's not something anyone would dare risk," said James, only half joking. The Marchioness of Shropshire may have been in her early seventies, but the Ton still looked to her for guidance on such matters.

"I don't think it will take long for Abby to win them all over anyway," said Henry. "She hasn't been in any sort of scrapes since they got married; at least, none that are of consequence! Besides, she makes Cousin Gloucester smile, and anyone who can do that will be able to bring the Ton to heel."

"I take it you like her, then?" asked James, and Henry turned her large brown eyes onto him.

"Very much, as I explained in my letters. The entire family descended on Gloucester House over Christmas, and she utterly charmed us all as the perfect hostess. Why, Grandpapa is still talking about the food that was served, and complains that our cook just cannot roast duck to the same high standard."

"Which reminds me, I must go and speak with cook about ordering some desserts from Gunters for our dinner party tomorrow," said the Marchioness as she got to her feet. "No, there's no need to leave on my account, Cottingham. You're practically family so I'm sure there can be no censure in you talking with Henrietta for another ten minutes. you can beg her leave to dance with you at the Loughcroft's ball this evening."

"I'm afraid I didn't receive an invitation," said James, not that he wanted one anyway. He was a wealthy bachelor in his mid-twenties, which meant that every ball he attended inevitably descended into a game of dodge-the-matchmakers who all seemed determined to shackle him to some dull, worthy girl who would bore him to tears within minutes.

"Nonsense my boy; your mother was invited, and naturally that extends to you as well. I shall inform Emma at dinner this evening that she is to expect you, and also arrange for a private supper next week so that you can regale us all with tales of Montreal."

The Marchioness clicked the library door shut behind her, and Henry shook her head in apparent amusement of the impropriety of the situation.

"For all the world as though we are still muddy children, and not of marriageable age!"

James smiled, glad that she could see the absurdity of the situation as well. "Should I remain in the hope that your Grandfather does not walk in the room and demand that I do the honourable thing?"

She glanced down at her hands. "Oh I could do much worse than marrying you, I suppose. At least you aren't going to start writing sonnets that compare my left earlobe to a tulip, or some such idiotic nonsense."

"You don't mean to tell me that some poor sop is so in love with you that he's resorted to poetry?"

For a moment it looked as though she was irritated by his comment, but the serene smile returned so quickly that James supposed he had imagined it.

"It's far worse than that, you know. I took pity on Herbert Filey a few weeks ago, because he's not very confident around ladies and the others can make dreadful fun of him. They started to mock his poetry when they learned he had dedicated some particularly awful verses to me, so I said I found them very pretty."

"And now?" he asked, a smile twitching on the corner of his lips.

She sighed. "Now they are all trying to outdo themselves by writing odes in my honour about everything from my grace and deportment to my perfect fingernails, and each one is worse than the last."

He let loose his laughter, unable to stop himself from remembering a younger version of Henry refusing to memorise Shakespeare's sonnets, and instead declaring the bard to be a prosy old bore.

"It isn't funny, you know. I know they all think it's a great joke, but it's a sad trial to me," she said, although she was smiling.

"My apologies, Henry. I had no idea of the problems a beautiful heiress must endure."

Her smile faltered, and although she didn't quite scowl, she looked decidedly mulish. "Don't be such a bore, James. You wouldn't find it much fun if your inamoratas all started writing poems about the shape of your nostrils, now would you?"

The image was a striking one, and James couldn't help but shudder at the thought. "Good God, no, but for a start, I do not have any inamoratas – and how the devil do you know anything about them, anyway?"

Henry waved a hand at nothing in particular. "Grandpapa was concerned you were running away to Canada with an opera dancer. And no, I have no idea where he picked up such a notion."

It took James a moment to collect himself before he could actually speak. "I don't think that you should speak so freely of such things in front of gentlemen, Henry."

She turned those wide eyes onto him again. "I can hardly influence what subjects Grandpapa chooses to discuss with me, James, but you are of course free to explain to him what are appropriate topics of conversation for him to share with his granddaughter."

James opened and closed his mouth a few times as a witty comeback refused to present itself, so he settled on a rueful smile instead. "Wretch! You don't change, do you?"

"On the contrary, I have it on good authority that I've changed a great deal in the last year."

James nodded. "Acquired some town bronze. Don't worry about that, Henry; I promise that you'll always be a hoydenish eight-year-old to my mud-splattered, twelve-year-old self."

"How reassuring," she replied, and he got the feeling that her smile didn't go more than surface deep.

In truth, she had changed since their carefree childhood spent romping across their respective estates and getting themselves into all manner of trouble. They'd been thick as thieves as children, as a mutual love of the outdoors and playing pranks had inevitably brought them together.

Then he'd been sent away to Eton, and she'd been schooled in the ways of being a Lady. She'd grown into pretty enough girl in her last three seasons, always dressed in modest white gowns and with her hair smoothed back to a bun at the nape of her neck. If there were times when he felt that her demure behaviour bordered on the insipid, he reminded himself that she was only adopting the fashionable air looked on approvingly by more established members of the Ton, and complimented her accordingly.

"Did you really not read my letters?" she blurted out without warning.

James sighed, and tugged once again at his cravat. He'd read each letter with pleasure as he'd received them, but for the life of him, he couldn't recall a single word that she'd written. He'd consumed them as though she was there beside him, telling him all of the gossip he'd missed, before he'd put them away and forgotten their contents in the day-to-day life of Montreal.

Somehow, he doubted she would be any more flattered by the truth than by her assumption that he'd never so much as broken the seal. If he'd had any sense at all he would have read them on the ship on his way back from Canada to remind him of what she'd said, but he'd been sick as a dog for most of the voyage and that was not something he wished to share with her, either.

"I'm sorry, Henry, but with my younger brother to set up and the investments to review, I suppose I simply forgot about them."

Her smile was tight. "No need to apologise again, James. It seems reasonable enough to expect you would be bored to tears by letters about my life."

"Never," he declared. "I'm desperate to learn everything that you've been up to while I've been gone."

"Nothing that you don't already know, I suppose. I am entering my fourth Season, and the tabbies are beginning to sharpen their claws. It is a great delight of theirs that even an heiress such as myself can reach twenty-one and still be unwed."

"But how is this?" asked James. "You've told me yourself that half the Ton is writing poetry celebrating the length of your eyelashes. Surely one or two of them have come up to scratch?"

"Four, actually."

"You're joking!" he found himself sputtering.

"Not in the least," replied Henry, the demure way she folded her hands into her lap defying the steel in her voice. "Two were gazetted fortune hunters, to be sure, but the others would not have been contemptible matches."

"Then why on earth would you not accept one of them?"

She gave a surprising elegant shrug, but looked over her shoulder and out of the window as she replied. "Because I want something more than that."

"Hanging out for a coronet, are you? A laudable enough goal I suppose, but I hope our friendship allows for me to be blunt and say that after three seasons it is unlikely for you to make a brilliant match."

She made a sound that could have been a laugh, or quite possibly a sob. "Very true, I daresay. However, I'm not holding out for a brilliant match, as I would very much like to marry for love."

James shook his head at the discovery that the mud-covered urchin of his youth had apparently gained a world view more suited to romantic novels. "I always thought you were smarter than that."

She turned to face him with a frown. "In what way?"

"That you were too intelligent to be swayed by this silly fashion for True Love and all that rot. I know you've somehow got it into your head that love will sweep you off your feet and be a grand adventure, but it doesn't happen that way for most people."

"It worked for my cousins; Emma married Loughcroft, and Gloucester just married Abby not eight months ago," she replied, looking mulish again.

James sighed. "They were the exception, and you know it. You said it yourself: you've been out for three seasons. Surely if you were going to fall head over heels in love with a worthy swain then it would have happened by this point. Marrying a good, kind gentleman for whom you feel affection is a much more realistic proposition."

Henry studied him for a moment, and he had the uncomfortable feeling that she was seeing him with new eyes and that neither of them would like what she found. "Is that all you want from a marriage, James? Kindness and affection?"

A strange sensation churned in his gut, although he had no words to describe it. "Isn't that what everyone wants?"

"No, some of us want more than that," she said with a sigh. "Besides, you are wrong about me. I am very much head over heels in love with a worthy gentleman."

James started at this revelation. "Good God, since when? And why haven't you told me before?"

"Because I've been hopelessly in love with him for an age," she replied, which for Henry could mean anything from five minutes to five months. "However, he has not shown the slightest inclination to court me despite much encouragement, so there's little point in hope."

Without thinking, James moved to his knees beside Henry's chair in order to capture her hand.

"Then the man you love is a fool who doesn't deserve you," he said softly, genuinely saddened that any man could think to break the heart of his lifelong friend.

Henry laughed, and the sound was bitter enough to remind him that she was more grown up than he sometimes remembered.

"I've told myself that often enough," she said. She stared forlornly into the fireplace for a moment, before giving herself a little shake. "Well, congratulations James, you've managed to accomplish something Grandmama never has."

He frowned at her. "What would that be?"

"Convinced me that I need to throw myself into this business of catching a husband."

James stood, knowing Henry too well to be surprised at her sudden change of heart, but disliking it all the same. "I never said you needed to throw yourself into it, precisely."

Henry held up a hand to silence him. "No, there is no need to harangue me further; I will consult with Grandmama and do my very best to be open to accepting the suit of some – how did you put it? – some kind gentleman that I can hold in mutual affection."

She clambered up to her feet with all the grace of a bear cub before smoothing the creases out of her dress. She did not look at him directly, and for the life of him James couldn't quite place the emotions that were dancing all across her face.

"You look like you are preparing yourself to face the gallows," he said, trying to joke with her. She lifted her large brown eyes to his once again, and for some unknown reason he felt his heart skip a beat.

"No, just the parson's mousetrap. I can count on your help during my search though, can I not?"

"My help?"

"Yes, in choosing a suitable husband. After all, you know me better than anyone save my grandparents, and Lord knows that they have shown some terrible judgement on this matter. Grandpapa insists on keeping copies of the poetry and swears he will grant his blessing to whoever comes up with the most entertaining verse."

"I-" for some unknown reason, words failed James completely as she stared at him with the type of trust that can only be formed over a lifetime of friendship. "I don't know how much use I would be."

She smiled. "Oh, I think you will prove extremely useful, and you can begin by thinking about which gentlemen of your acquaintance are seeking marriage. I don't mind if the man in question is poor so long as he has birth and looks to recommend him, but no fortune hunters. Somehow I doubt they will remain kind and affectionate once my dowry is placed into their hands. Now, I will have to shoo you out so that I can go and tell Grandmama that I am willing and ready to get myself leg-shackled."

James found himself being unceremoniously hurried out to the hallway, where the Shropshire's butler was already waiting for him with his hat and gloves. "I say, Henry, this is starting to sound awfully like one of your queer starts."

"Nonsense, husband-hunting is a perfectly acceptable pastime for a woman of my age and rank," she told him with a dazzling smile. "And who better to help me out than my childhood best friend? If we rub along together famously, then surely I could find affection with one of your male friends as well?"

None that he would not have to call out immediately afterwards, James told himself, and was then surprised at the violence of his own thoughts.

"I suppose-"

"Excellent! You may have the supper dance with me at the Loughcroft's ball tonight – you know Grandmama will never forgive you if you don't go, don't you? – and then during supper you can let me know who you think might make me a good husband," said Henry, her eyes bright for some reason he could not explain.

James wanted to say something to reassure her, for he was observant enough to know that she was upset and worried that his well-intentioned words had upset her, but before he knew precisely what had happened he found himself on the front steps of the Shropshire's Mayfair home as the butler firmly – but respectfully – closed the door in his face.

"Help Henry find a husband?" he said to himself with a faint trace of disgust. For some reason, he could not find any enthusiasm for the task at all.

The Foolish Friend is available to purchase now!

Made in the USA
Middletown, DE
25 May 2019